PROFESSIONAL MADNESS

PETER KENNEDY

ISBN-13: 9798494590091

CONTENTS

CHAPTER 1

THE CARING DOCTOR

Everyone plays a role in life. They may not always be aware of it, but, in reality, they do it all the time. People such as doctors, judges, politicians, and newscasters invariably have two separate lives. There is the professional persona they want the world to see, which has a set of ground rules, regulations, and proscriptions that allows them to survive in their jobs, perhaps gain universal respect and pay the bills. Then there is the personal life that only a few people ever see, and this is almost always completely different from their role as a professional. Here there are seldom any limits to good behaviour and the hard reality is that just about anything goes at home or when hidden from public view. The notion of 'what you see is what you get' is manifest nonsense. No-one really believes that is ever the case. We seldom show our real selves. But there is another level of this duality of living, and this is the one that many of us either deny or are just unaware of. It is the process of invariable self-deception where we are forced to play another role in our personal lives, one that allows us to survive the traumas of everyday living and avoid the absolute act of self-termination. That is of course a euphemism for suicide, the end of life that we are never allowed to talk about freely. In our own little world of reality, an existence that frankly can be just too painful to bear, we adopt a role for ourselves that somehow shields us from life's traumas and the daily stress that sometimes results from the sheer labour of our own thinking. This can be confused with or even identified as *amour propre* or self-respect, but it is not that at all. It is something different. It is an imaginary wall that we create, usually unconsciously, that allows us to play a role in our personal lives that helps to keeps us on the rails. It is different from the professional role because that is generally a deliberate mask that we are forced to wear out of a sense of duty and necessity. We are generally aware of and complicit in that role even though it may be imposed on us by others from above. But the role we play at home or when not in a workplace is one that is part of our intrinsic mental apparatus and has no rules or regulations. So, the problem we have to consider is what happens when we become so aware of our two roles – the professional and the personal – that they become completely disrupted. More serious is the inevitable disintegration of a person's grip on life, even their sanity, when the personal role that we adopt as a matter of necessity moves from the unconscious to the conscious realm.

Then there is no predicting the outcome as everyone has the potential to become mad in their own particular way. This naturally can cause great distress and inconvenience to everyone.

*

Paul Sellner-Smith is feeling particularly pleased with himself, and that is not a very frequent phenomenon. An eminent cancer specialist, or clinical oncologist to be medically precise, he knows he has used and demonstrated his consummate skills several times already this Tuesday morning in the hospital outpatient clinic. While long inured to the typical flattery and rather moving gratitude that many patients and their families show to him as the eminent 'Professor', nevertheless he has retained a keen sense of his own worth as a very effective and meticulous doctor. In his exulted role as a Professor of Oncology at a top London teaching hospital, there can be few cancer specialists in the United Kingdom who can match his all-round abilities and wide knowledge of medicine and biology. He also has a keen and sensitive appreciation of the dreadful and very real fears of so many of his unfortunate patients, but that level of empathy and sensitivity is almost a *sine qua non* for doctors in his medical specialty. Despite the positive external perception of his professional abilities by both patients and many, but, it has to be said, not all of his colleagues, Paul has still managed to retain a degree of apparent humility. But sometimes he has to work a bit on that. There is a subtle difference between modesty and humility. While privately lacking the former, he shows definite signs of the latter, at least to the outside world. He is a man who plays the professional role rather better than most. But in his position, there is really no other choice.

*

His patient tally was six that morning, which is about par for the course. Three were completely new referrals from medical colleagues and three were patients already under his care and who needed to be closely monitored, especially as one of them was part of an important clinical trial of a novel anti-cancer drug. Every one of them required his careful attention to detail and total concentration. Sometimes things can go wrong because the cancer progresses in spite of treatment, and at other times the patient becomes physically compromised because of the side effects of the drugs themselves, and he always has to be on the lookout for both which, of course, are not mutually exclusive. He doesn't believe in the benign and wise power of 'mother nature' and the body's natural healing powers. In fact, he has never had faith in any of that nonsense, even when a young medical student. He has always been acutely aware of the unpredictability and fragility of life, and in most cases whether or not a person gets cancer is just down to random mutations in the life's genetic code. Of course, like most doctors he preaches to everyone about the wisdom of a healthy life style and advises against such things as smoking, drinking excessive alcohol, obesity, and an unhealthy diet. But in his heart he thinks that when your number is up then there's virtually nothing you can do about it. That's just life, or, more accurately, that's just death prolonged.

He is a fatalist in that sense but behaves nevertheless like the ultimate optimist. After all, what else can he be in his job? Besides, he knows that over the years his treatment has prolonged many lives and has occasionally even cured some of them. He always gets a genuine buzz of pleasure and satisfaction when that happens, so his heart is probably in the right place. But, as will be seen, the same cannot be said about his brain.

*

An important attribute Paul has always possessed is the ability to empathise with people who have had the misfortune to become ill through no fault of their own. 'No one gets away in life free' is a maxim once uttered by a very sick patient of his many years before when he was just a fledgling specialist. *How true that is,* he thinks, a statement so simple and short but nevertheless one that expresses what must surely be a universal reality applicable to virtually everyone who has the good fortune to be alive. However hard he tries, Paul is unable to think of anyone he has ever met during his forty-nine years of existence on the planet who has emerged completely unscathed by life's cruelties – some subtle and slight while others are cruel and devastating. He himself has had to endure the pain and grief of both parental loss and betrayal by people whom he had trusted implicitly, but so far at least he had only experienced relatively minor physical ailments and not the physical horrors of malignant disease. But he also knows that mental horrors can be as devastating as physical infirmities, though the former are perhaps more likely to improve with time than the latter. *Maybe*, he thinks. Time can wound just as well as it can heal.

*

Sometimes he is truly terrified by the random nature of serious disease, and cancer is certainly no exception. But some of the diseases his neurological colleagues have to deal with, like motor neurone disease, which is truly awful, are probably even worse since they are always relentless in their progression and are essentially untreatable. The whole scenario is like a card game or the random throwing of a pair of dice, and it is purely a matter of chance as to whether one is allowed to live as a lucky survivor or condemned to illness and death as an unlucky loser. For sure, a dangerous environment or risky occupation can sometimes exert a strong influence on the chances of getting cancer, and a minority of these malignant conditions have a strong hereditary component, but in the great majority of cases it is just a question of luck. Bad luck would be a better description. How often has Paul been asked by a stricken and newly diagnosed patient or their close relatives why they have been singled out for such cruel punishment? And how frequently has he been asked by a patient the simple question: 'Why me?' That is a perfectly legitimate question. The problem is in the answer.

*

Naturally, he has never found the perfect answer to that perennial and entirely predictable question, but somehow, he has always managed to respond in a compassionate, if not slightly philosophical, way. Each answer is ever so slightly different, and instinctively tailored to the individual person. In reality, a secret known only to himself, he considers only one true answer which is that it is just a question of luck. The whole scenario is just fortuitous. Since he doesn't believe in God, he never feels the need to invoke the divine intervention of a supreme deity, and even if that were actually the case then he feels it would not say much for the supposed benign and compassionate nature of an all-powerful being. Paul lost his religious faith many years ago, a loss that was powerfully reinforced by all the suffering he had then witnessed as a cancer doctor. While he sometimes envies those who possess a strong religious faith, he feels more comfortable with his coming to terms with what he thinks is the stark truth, namely that when you are dead you are dead, and no more. Perhaps that explains why he sets great store by human life. That is a rather interesting philosophical question. Paul reckons that our lives, and the way we live them, are defined as much by the inevitability of death as by what we actually achieve, or at least try to achieve.

*

It is just after midday, and he decides to delay his patient dictation until he has finished lunch which as usual is sparse in the extreme. No wonder he is so slim. Some people think he is deliberately punishing himself by such minor starvation, but for Paul it is just a matter of staying healthy. Anyway, that's what he tells himself, somewhat unconvincingly. As he sits in his surprisingly small hospital office and wolfs his low-fat yoghurt, ripe banana, and black coffee in five minutes flat, he thinks about the morning's patients. One in particular had formed a strong impression which he could not get out of his mind, much as that might go against his professional attitude and persona. While this young woman shows little difference from so many of his unfortunate patients and embodies a common medical challenge that he is supremely qualified to deal with, there was something about her wan appearance and brave acceptance of the cancer diagnosis that just struck him as tragic. This individual empathy and acute level of compassion is something he has experienced a few times during his career, invariably unpredictable and especially towards the very vulnerable, but in this case he just felt he should try even harder than usual to allay her underlying fear of her terrifying disease and inevitable extinction. What she doesn't yet know is that the treatment regime he has in mind for her, consisting of intensive chemotherapy but no surgery at this late stage, one which offers the best chance of improvement, maybe even a remission, is in some ways even worse to bear than the disease itself. How often is that the case in medicine, he wonders? It's called the quality of life.

*

Sharon was just twenty-nine years old, was married with two toddler children, a boy and a girl, and until a month before had been working part-time as a secretary in a well-known legal firm. She was rather young to have ovarian cancer, but Paul knows by now that anything can happen to anyone and anywhere. She had been referred to him by one of his medical colleagues in gastroenterology. She had a number of worrying symptoms that had initially been attributed by her general practitioner to the irritable bowel syndrome, but when the more detailed investigations had been carried out his colleague's worst fear had been correct.

Despite the relative paucity of symptoms such as abdominal bloating, mild lower abdominal pain and urinary frequency, the tests showed that she had in reality ovarian cancer with convincing evidence of some spread to the liver, and just possibly to the lungs. So, she had metastatic ovarian cancer that had already advanced rapidly though it has presented late to the doctors. The real clue to the true diagnosis had been the effortless and considerable weight loss over the previous three months. That was a 'red flag' if ever there was one. *Poor woman,* he thinks to himself. Why do these awful things nearly always happen to the nicest people? It must be the luck of the dice, the random strike that has no ethical attachment whatsoever. But why is life so incredibly unfair? It is enough to make one very cynical indeed. But life and time have already damaged Paul despite the powerful exterior that he shows to the outside world. His true nature is soft and vulnerable despite the hard carapace of his professional self.

*

When explaining her illness to Sharon, what has been found on the tests, and how he intends to treat her, Paul demonstrates all that has made him such a respected figure in the oncology world. While explaining the facts of her case and the range of possible survival times, he is careful to give her as much hope as he can and points out that she may well be one of the fortunate 'outliers' who manage to survive for many years. One must never take away hope. Without that it just isn't possible to carry on, whether or not one is very ill. He is surprised by her exceptionally calm demeanour and impressive equanimity, but he has the insight to know that this is likely to be just the outward showing of a brave face to him. She is an intelligent and knowledgeable young woman and knows full well what all this means and what is in store for her over the ensuing months and maybe years if she is lucky, or, for that matter, unlucky. Paul can visualise all too well the complete, but probably temporary, breakdown of her personality this terrible event must cause, and has the insight to imagine the type of conversation she will have later at home with her husband, and the emotional pain she will feel as she picks up and caresses her two little children. But he shows her none of this. He knows he mustn't. He does not hold with the increasing tendency of younger medical doctors to display all their emotions to their stricken patients, the so-called medical professionals who think nothing of shedding empathetic tears in front of them. Paul is a student from the older school and all his tears are unshed. He will save his deepest emotions for later when he gets home.

*

Home should be a haven for people like Paul. But in reality, it has become more akin to purgatory. That is partly his fault due to his increasing mental instability, but both he and Jane, his insightful, but in some ways somewhat unsympathetic wife of twenty years, still holds out the hope that their domestic life is still salvageable and may yet be prevented from descending into a form of hell. Much of Jane's apparent insensitivity to Paul's state of mind is really a form of protection, both for him and also for her, driven by the forlorn and misguided hope that by trying to ignore many of his increasing eccentricities they may somehow resolve spontaneously, and normal behaviour will be resumed as soon as possible. That is wishful thinking, and is doomed to failure, an outcome made more likely by his unwillingness to confront his frighteningly erratic behaviour and reluctance to recognise the real reasons for his bizarre mental state. No-one in his workplace had the slightest notion of Paul's true mental state. Besides, they all had other priorities.

After finishing their typically light supper of fish and vegetables, Paul and Jane have a brief but cold and impersonal discussion about the kind of day he's had at the hospital after which he sits alone in his study, his private citadel where he can think anything he wants. He needs to make some sense of all that has happened to both him and his patients, but before he will allow himself to do that, he feels compelled by some outside entity to see his two young children, the seven-year-old Charlotte and the younger Gavin who is just five. So, he quietly opens the doors of his children's bedrooms where he observes in turn the gentle undulating movements of their sleeping bodies, no doubt engrossed within their childlike dreams yet still oblivious to the traumas of the outside world. How long will this blissful ignorance last? He smiles at their apparent innocence and unsullied souls and then closes each door gently as he consciously excludes these placid visions from his troubled mind.

*

He now allows time for reflection, or more accurately, morbid rumination. As he sits back in his black study swivel chair in his small square study lined with hundreds of books scattered along wooden shelves and sequestered in every available corner, his mind focuses again on the three new patients he had seen that morning at the hospital. All three of them had cancer. The first was a newly diagnosed middle-aged man of sixty-two years with a kidney tumour which mercifully had been detected at an early stage before any obvious spread. But he will reserve judgement on the likely prognosis until he sees the histology report in case it shows the more worrying sarcomatous changes. But for this man he is hopeful. The second patient had lung cancer and he was a long-time smoker of 40 cigarettes a day for about thirty-five years. This poor man of fifty-five had a number of suspicious looking areas in his liver so he probably has metastatic spread already. More tests would be required to be sure, but he just hoped he would tolerate and respond to chemotherapy. His medical colleagues had been remarkably thorough already in their investigations before they referred their patient to him. Then there was this unfortunate, if not tragic, young woman with disseminated advanced stage ovarian cancer. In the outpatient clinic he was the ultimate professional, but here back at home and alone with his thoughts he asks himself why life is so unfair.

*

Like so many medical doctors, Paul is a hypochondriac. The only difference from most people with this particular mindset is that as a physician he has the required knowledge and resources to convince himself that he's relatively healthy. True as that may be, it does not detract from the suffering he endures as he fears that he has contracted just about every disease that he encounters. It all started as a young medical student when he was convinced he had throat cancer. He was only disabused of this after seeing a leading ear, nose, and throat specialist who was kindness itself and thought Paul's throat discomfort was actually due to a post-nasal drip which was worse at night. Following this he convinced himself over the years that he had so many ailments that the number would probably fill a book. But now he was almost fifty years old, what was once just an illogical fear has become an increasingly reality, He finds that pretty scary. But since he has never lost any weight over the previous four years, he never thought it likely that he was suffering from any form of lurking cancer. He did sometimes wonder, however, about such conditions as autoimmune disease and Multiple Sclerosis. Unlikely but still possible, he reckons.

But all of this physical worry counts for nothing compared with the disease of his mind, one which he has only become increasingly but also vaguely aware of during recent months. The more deeply he thinks about it, the less sure he is of his abilities as a doctor. While never a particularly confident person, which is illogical since he is both highly successful professionally and also very good looking, he is now completely convinced he's a fake. He isn't an imposter as such, but he feels he is not the person everyone thinks he is. He does not loathe himself. He just thinks he is a complete failure. He has failed as a doctor, an academic, a person, a husband, and a father. In fact, he finds it difficult to even justify his very existence. He has naturally thought seriously about taking his own life, but for now that is an option for the future and not an immediate necessity. Whatever else people, including his wife, who clearly means well, may think about him, he considers himself to be a complete 'waste of space' as the popular epithet goes. Along with this profoundly negative view of himself, he has not tried to resist the temptation to think badly of just about everyone and everything around him. He is perfectly entitled to hate himself but that does not give him justification for thinking ill of others. While that is a logical and ethical view, unfortunately neither logic nor ethics plays an important role in Paul's current thinking or world view. They certainly should, but they don't.

He knows he has an important part to play in the management of some of the world's most seriously ill people, and he is prepared and happy to fulfil that professional commitment. That is what he has been trained for all his life and, despite his increasing irrationality, he has still retained a strong sense of duty. He reckons that will be the last human emotion to go. It is ingrained within his core and is literally part of his DNA. But that doesn't stop him feeling animosity towards some of the people who are referred to him. He recalls hearing a disturbing conversation several years previously, when he was still a trainee, between a patient due to see him and her accompanying friend.

"Just remember," her friend said quietly to her, "you should see this as a financial opportunity."

When Paul heard this, as had one of his most trusted senior nursing colleagues, he experienced a surge of anger that he had to work hard to suppress and hide. He decided to be even more careful than usual, treated the patient with great, if not exaggerated respect, and faithfully documented everything he did. Unsurprisingly he did not detect any evidence of disease after extensive investigation. Then two weeks after her discharge from hospital he received a large buff envelope containing an intimidating letter from her solicitor accusing him of medical negligence and not diagnosing her underlying serious illness. There was also a demand for financial compensation for the time lost due to both her illness and the time in hospital. After a period of eight months and several exchanges of letters between her solicitor and his medical defence organisation, the matter was finally dropped. But this was not before he felt he'd been put through the mill and was made much more cynical than before. So, his colleagues may say, this was an isolated case and most atypical of the vast majority of patients. While he agreed that was very likely to be true, nevertheless it left him scarred and wary, if not somewhat defensive in his general approach to medicine. In reality this person had chosen the very last doctor in the hospital to target for what was in effect a cynical form of attempted extortion. He has had at least two further encounters of this kind since then but always managed to win the argument. He is just too careful.

*

So why should Paul be permanently affected by such dreadful, albeit very rare, behaviour? The vast majority of patients would never dream of behaving badly in this way, and most of his colleagues would put it down to just being part of the job, something that all doctors have to deal with. That is also true, but Paul is not everyone and takes all such things personally. Not every doctor has the ability to be robust. What really disturbs him most is the inexorable feeling of hate that he feels towards these people who are out to hurt him. And even when he is successful in his rebuttals he is still hurt and damaged in some way. Even worse, this feeling of hate is almost enjoyable in its naked severity. Surely that can't be normal?

It is said that you always hurt the one you love. Paul never set out to hurt anyone, least of all any member of his family. Let's be clear – we are not talking about physical injury, but more a subtle change in attitude towards everyone living in his home so that they are made to suffer through indirect means. Unfortunately, that also includes Paul himself. Whether or not he is a kind of narcissist with an unrealistically high regard for himself, something that is pretty unlikely, the end result nevertheless is that he decimates the lives of everyone close to him, and that, of course, includes himself.

CHAPTER 2

THE APPARENT KINDNESS OF COLLEAGUES

If you work as a medical specialist in a hospital or a family doctor's practice, then it is vital to have a group of good supportive colleagues. In principle, that is. Doctors are like everyone else and possess all the usual weaknesses and foibles of human beings. What tends to mark them out from others is their specialised medical knowledge based on many years of student and junior doctor training, and also of course their adherence to a strict professional code. But what they sometimes tend to forget is that the code and behaviour mandated by their professional regulators applies to their fellow doctors as well as their admittedly vulnerable patients.

Paul had always been a well-nigh impeccable

colleague who could be guaranteed to provide the greatest possible support to any of the other cancer specialists who found themselves temporarily deployed to another hospital service, or else had to take sick leave for whatever reason, whether that was physical or psychological. He showed a great deal of empathy towards his fellow physicians, and particularly so to the young trainee doctors whom he took turns in supervising. He himself had been badly bullied by a few of his senior medical bosses during his early training, and because of this unpleasant past experience he made a point of being exceptionally kind and considerate to his junior staff. Besides, as the old adage says, 'one should always be nice to those on the way up as you want them to be nice to you when you are on the way down'. Time and time again he has witnessed the sad truth of that golden rule. Because of his unfailing kindness towards them, as well as his obvious eminence in his specialty, all the junior doctors in his unit were extremely fond of him, and this was to be one of his greatest problems. Things were not helped in this regard by his exceptional teaching skills at all levels. He still participated in the general acute admission on-call rota which, frankly, he loathed both because of its unpredictability and the outside chance that he might not know how to deal with an acutely ill patient. In reality that was always very unlikely because, to put it in a nutshell, he was just a very good physician as well as a top-notch medical oncologist. He only learned at a relatively late stage of his career that it was always rather dangerous to be too good at his job, and even more so to be so popular amongst the juniors. One of his American colleagues once said to him, 'No good turn goes unpunished', and, unfortunately, he had a valid point. He so wishes that was not true.

When did he become aware of the precariousness of his position, one that he perceived as totally secure? It was more an insidious awareness in the early stages, with clear clues as to what might eventually happen. Only later would it all explode in his face.

Paul sometimes recalls a period in his life working for the worst medical bully that he ever knew, one who was never happy if his junior staff had done everything right. By doing that it was, naturally, certainly very good for the patients but unfortunate for the juniors as it left his boss with nothing to complain about. So, he and his colleagues devised an interesting, if not rather eccentric, coping strategy which was to make one deliberate but minor mistake in each case. They would deliberately fail to carry out a minor blood test that they knew their boss favoured in all cases. Once he had upbraided them during the main ward round for their disgraceful investigational omission he would be satisfied and calm down. He had no idea that he himself was being manipulated by the very people he thought he had power over.

While Paul was equally, if not more, obsessional in his attention to detail than this awful man, it was unthinkable that he would ever be in the remotest bit harsh with his young staff.

The really big and totally unexpected problem with some of his so-called colleagues arose out of the blue as a result of relatively minor misunderstanding among his young laboratory staff, none of whom were medical. But from small beginnings come major events, so the old wisdom tells us.

Paul is a serious scientist as well as a clinician and runs a hospital laboratory overseen by a super-efficient technician with over twenty years' experience, and five enthusiastic junior staff. Being a careful and rather obsessional academic, he checks all the experimental results of his young colleagues very carefully before any scientific paper is let outside the laboratory and submitted to a peer-reviewed journal. His real expertise lies in the field of brain tumours, especially the very malignant ones that don't respond at all well to any treatment. That's important work as just about everyone would agree. After the completion of one of his group's research projects, which had been carried out by two young scientists in his laboratory, he was shown the draft paper together with all of the 'raw data' consisting of graphs, photographs, and electrophoretic gels. The project involved the study of a set of proteins which were analysed for any significant biochemical changes after their interaction with cultured human tumour cells. How relevant to actual human disease was as yet uncertain but he, and also the granting agency which funded the work, certainly thought the study was well worth doing. It was certainly cutting-edge research.

*

As Paul carefully scrutinised the data, he slowly realised that something was wrong. The conclusions seemed reasonable enough but the pattern of protein alteration on the gels just didn't seem right to him. When two of the key protein images were transposed the whole picture made sense to him. He concluded that almost certainly there had been an unintentional mistake made by his PhD student and post-doctoral scientist. These things happen sometimes, and he was convinced this was due to 'pilot error' and was not deliberate. Accordingly, he met with his two young colleagues and went over the data and conclusions and told them what he thought had happened. They all spent about an hour checking what had been done and indeed one of the protein gels had been inadvertently misaligned though not mislabelled. It was indeed a mistake but no more than that. It was very fortunate that Paul knew his stuff so well and was so vigilant, but after all that was his job. He is the eminent Professor and laboratory chief and he just carried out 'due diligence'. Though he was kind and totally reassuring to his colleagues, they were both, understandably, devastated. The student, a young woman from Belgium, burst into tears of anguish and was furious with herself, and the more senior scientist, a young man from London, went very quiet and extremely pale while all the time shaking his head in disbelief that such a mistake could be made and what might have happened. After all, he was able to see the big picture as was his boss who might well think less of him after this. Paul just knew from their reaction that the mistake was just that and not more insidious. He actually felt more sorrow for them rather than irritation and concern at what might have transpired had erroneous data been published, though he had little doubt that the journal reviewers would have picked this up. But Paul is no fool. He tells them to repeat the whole experiment to confirm what he thinks had happened.

They did this very carefully, and ten days later Paul was shown the experimental results which confirmed precisely that his interpretation of the experiment was correct. All three of them were more than relieved. The paper was suitably rewritten and then sent off to the journal to wait for the customary four to six weeks to receive the editor's verdict. No harm was done, but it was still a near miss for sure. Most definitely, Paul had handled a tricky situation with textbook competence and integrity.

Paul had just assumed that he would hear no more of this, and he certainly hadn't discussed it with anyone. Unfortunately, he assumed wrongly. He did not know how this episode got out to his clinical colleagues, but it certainly did. The first time he became aware of a problem was three days after the paper submission when one of his closest clinical colleagues, a genial scot called Marcus McBurny, who was also a University Professor, quietly took him aside in one of the hospital's long corridors and told him that two of their clinical colleagues were discussing an apparent 'scandal' in his laboratory that was going to be very bad news for Paul. He explained in unusually passionate terms to Marcus what had actually happened and that there was no truth whatsoever in what these two, clearly malignant, men were discussing. Marcus totally believed him but warned him of the danger. Unfortunately for Paul, one of the two consultants involved was one of his very few enemies who had been out to get him for years. This man, who was called Robert Grisaldo, was in Paul's view a failed academic, an astute clinician, and a thoroughly nasty piece of work who deeply resented his great success and stellar career. Interestingly, all the junior staff members were very afraid of Dr Grisaldo who was essentially a vain bully with a natural academic talent as small as his ego was large. In all fairness, however, Paul thought he was quite a good doctor. It was probably more a question of resentment than jealousy, but it was also the case that the enmity was felt on both sides.

*

Over a period of an hour Paul's mood changed from one of bemused acceptance of his colleagues' stupidity to one of increasing alarm as he realised just how dangerous such talk could be, especially if followed up by some kind of action against him. The fact that he was completely innocent of any subterfuge or wrongdoing whatsoever made little difference to the rapidly escalating situation as all that seemed to matter was an external perception of a misdemeanour. Even colleagues whom he had always regarded as loyal seemed to look at him askance and sadly shake their heads at what was clearly heading for a minor scandal.

Paul made a vow to himself to never forget what these people had done to him, either through their cowardly inaction or active muckraking. He realised that his previous opinion of some of his colleagues was just too positive. That said, Marcus was unquestionably on his side, as were three of the other twelve colleagues, one of whom was, fortunately for Paul, the NHS head of the Oncology department, and the other two were both women for whom he had always had a very high regard. Both of them were furious with the sheer nastiness and ludicrous nature of the allegations. All four of these colleagues believed everything he told them about the incident, and he made a mental note of their loyalty and kindness toward him. But just as the situation was beginning to get seriously out of hand with this Grisaldo character loudly threatening to report Paul to the General Medical Council no less, a professional regulatory body with great power and also the ability to put the fear of God into even atheistic medical practitioners, he decided to take positive action and take control of the situation.

*

It thus transpired that just two days after the ugly rumours and 'Chinese Whispers' began to circulate, Paul somehow managed to terminate the frightening situation with a powerful combination of outrage and cool logic, supplemented with a whiff of menace towards the evil perpetrators of the lies. It was a regrettable performance but a necessary one, completely out of character for him, but one that had the great merit of success. The critical point to get across to all his colleagues was that the idea of 'no smoke without fire' was nonsense in his case.

He decided to call a special emergency meeting of the entire oncology staff, both NHS and University academic, and to directly confront his accusers. So, at exactly 1.00 p.m., eleven out of the twelve consultants, including the two ringleaders, gathered together in their common room and gave the floor to Paul. He sensed a curious mood of anticipation in the room, not unlike the imagined sight of an expectant audience waiting for a battle between gladiators who are trained to fight each other to the death. Well, he certainly resolved to fight hard to clear his good name, even though the whole situation was utterly ludicrous. He started by telling everyone that he was aware of the vicious and totally untrue rumours about his research work, and then spent five minutes explaining exactly what happened. Most of his colleagues nodded their heads and indicated their gratitude for his clear explanation, indicating that they were totally satisfied. No-one asked him any questions. Paul also told them that they should feel free to interview his two young junior scientists, and he also passed around a detailed minute that he had taken the trouble to write, recording all the meetings he'd had with them. More mild noises of general approval and thanks followed, but nothing was said by his two arch enemies who were as quiet as a couple of frightened mice. Clearly, they were trying it on with him in the hope that some dirt might stick, but all that emerged was evidence of their maliciousness and cowardice, both of which had some kind of resentment of him as their driving force. Paul then delivered the final blow when he named his two accusers and told them publicly to their face that he would not hesitate to sue them for slander if they uttered another negative word about him, and that they would also forfeit their honorary University titles if they pursued this non-event. Furthermore, he told all his colleagues that he had the full backing of the University lawyers and the Dean of the Medical School. He never heard another word from anyone about this matter after that point. However, Paul had a very long memory and would never forgive them, however childish that might seem to some. But that is his nature, and he was surprised at how vindictive he felt after being put through the mill in this way.

*

Later that evening at home he sat back in his favourite armchair and thought about the near disaster that had clearly been averted. He came to the conclusion that there is seldom any justice in life, and that the world is largely, but not entirely, crazy. But that is hardly a novel realisation as he himself knew. The critical issue is that this was something that was done by some of his colleagues to him, so he had learned this life lesson the hard way, and also relatively late in life. He really must be a rather naïve man despite his high intelligence to be in the remotest bit surprised by this classical example of human behaviour. A few people are just bad, a few are consistently good, and most individuals in the middle between these two extremes can be good or bad depending on the prevailing circumstances, in particular those with the capacity to harm them or displace them from their comfortable perches. No, he should certainly not be surprised. Several years previously, during the terrible global coronavirus pandemic of 2020-2022, he had seen many examples of mind-bogging stupidity and nastiness in his fellow humans, not to mention the despotism and controlling behaviour of the nation's misleading politicians, but at least there was a clear explanation for all that he had observed in people during that period. In the current situation the brush with potential disaster came upon him without any warning. He then decided for sure that, on balance, he despised the rest of the human race. At this point, however, he did not despise himself. All in good time.

What had happened to the notion of collegiality? As far as Paul was concerned this was a just a myth and only appeared to be a reality when everything in a social system was running smoothly. If the slightest link in an apparently stable collegial structure is somehow broken or even damaged, then the whole edifice just cracks open, and opposing factions will try to tear each other apart in an inevitably wounding free for all. What is perhaps a little strange is that Paul believes this with absolute certainty and entertains no doubts whatsoever. He may hate the entire human race, but now he hates his so-called colleagues even more. For the very idea of collegiality, he has nothing but absolute contempt. This is what they have done to him.

But like so many disillusioned and frustrated people, especially highly successful men it has to be admitted, Paul allows his hideously severe anger to spill over to his family, something that any fair-minded person would feel is totally unwarranted. Unfortunately, there is nothing fair minded or reasonable about Professor Paul Sellner-Smith when it comes to his personal and domestic life.

After a typically excellent evening meal of grilled salmon, asparagus, courgettes, and black beans washed down with a glass of fine red wine, one which Paul would never take for granted, he pours out the day's events to his wife Jane. He does this more in the form of a continuous rant rather than a balanced narrative, and this aptly reflects his inner rage at his so-called colleagues. While their marriage has continued to be a relatively stable one, at least by most conventional standards, there have been escalating tensions brought about by his steadily deteriorating mental state. He has discarded his professional persona as a top cancer specialist now that he is no longer in the toxic workplace, but he still clings to what he sees as his private dignity, his self-identification as a man of the world with a family and a home.

The following is a brief snapshot of one of their conversations at that time.

Jane: Why do you let these people get you down so much?

Paul: Because of what they tried to do. They're beneath contempt.

Jane: But they're just not worth it. Anyway, they just resent you—

Paul: No, they're jealous, not resentful. Jealous of what I've achieved in life.

Jane: I disagree. They resent you because of your energy and power, nothing else. It's wrong to think it's all about jealousy. It isn't.

Paul: Maybe you're right … I just don't know … actually I'm so sick of the whole business that I just don't care anymore.

Jane: Oh I think you do. Otherwise, you wouldn't be so upset still.

At this point Paul puts his head in his hands and remains silent for about thirty seconds while Jane looks on sympathetically. Eventually he looks up, his eyes red and tired.

Paul: Yes, I guess you're right about that too … sometimes I feel too disillusioned with the whole work thing to carry on.

Jane: Don't say that. You're better than all of them. They think you have everything – brilliance, good looks, power, high status, and they just resent you. You are a constant reminder of their pathetic mediocrity.

Paul: That's kind of you to say that. I disagree but you could well be right. They should see it from my side!

Jane: I know what you mean, but unfortunately these losers are seeing it from their side.

Paul: Oh, I don't think they see themselves as losers. I'm sure they aren't that insightful.

Jane: The problem is that they do see themselves in that way, especially when they compare themselves with you. It's a question of reality for them … no insight is necessary. You must see it that way and not take it all so personally.

Paul: It all sounds pretty personal to me.

Jane: See it as their problem, not yours. You have to rise above it. You need to live.

Paul: You mean I'm not really living right now?

Jane: Of course you are, in a biological sense. But in terms of living in the moment and enjoying being alive I honestly don't think you are. Maybe you should change your mindset.

Paul: Ah that's very topical, isn't it? I hear my wife, the clinical psychologist, speaking—

Jane: And what's wrong with that, may I ask?

Paul: Nothing at all. I just don't like being lectured to and being told what to do. By the way, I may be married to you but I'm not one of your bloody psychology patients.

Jane: Of course not. I'm giving you my best advice. Whether or not you actually take it is entirely up to you.

Paul: I see.

Jane: Do you? Good. I just don't like seeing you so upset and suffering like this.

Paul: Well, the emergency seems to be over, at least for now, but I'm sure those two bastards will try something again the moment they see a potential chink in my armour.

Jane: Actually, I rather doubt that, but best to be on your guard and keep a close eye on them.

Paul: I'll certainly do that, but you never know

when trouble is about to happen. Maybe this was just a warning shot.

Jane: Perhaps, but I suspect you scared the shit out of them and right now they're probably far more scared of you than you are of them.

Paul: I'm not scared of them at all. I just hate their guts.

Jane: They don't deserve your hate. The only person who's getting hurt is you. Just forget about it and get on with life.

Paul: I guess you're right, but that's easier said than done.

Jane: You have to put it behind you. All you have to do is forgive, but never forget.

Paul: All I have to do is stay alive. That will be the hardest part for sure.

CHAPTER 3

THE GRANDEST OF ROUNDS

Shortly after the laboratory affair that never was, Paul noted the time of 10.55 a.m. on his expensive Tag Heuer watch tightly strapped to his left wrist and briskly made his way along the long hospital corridor to the 'A' wing lecture theatre. Since it was a Wednesday morning it meant that the weekly hospital grand round, in which different clinical teams present their most 'interesting' cases to their junior and senior colleagues, would take place. The notion of interesting was invariably good for the doctor but bad news for the patient in question. He always rather enjoyed these rounds, and being a particularly well-trained and acute clinician, he almost always worked out the patient's diagnosis within the first few minutes of the presentation. On occasion a junior member of staff would only present a review of an important or rare condition, but usually the attendees were faced with a difficult case that was invariably a challenge to their diagnostic acumen. Paul just couldn't help being vocal in his always perceptive and penetrating comments and questions, followed by his usual correct diagnosis even though he knew in his heart that this infuriated some of his clinical colleagues while it clearly delighted some of the others, especially the numerous junior members of staff. For some reason he always got on particularly well with the neurologists in the hospital, and also quite well with the cardiologists, and he reckoned this mutual affability probably reflected a common respect for intellectual endeavour and prowess.

*

Soon after one of the cardiac registrars started her presentation, one which struck Paul as being particularly slick and professional, he noticed out of the corner of his right eye that his would-be nemesis, none other than Dr Robert Grisaldo, was sitting just five seats away from him in the same row. They both avoided any suggestion of eye contact which was fine with him. Then, somewhat out of character, Paul's attention started to drift away from the case being presented as he began to contemplate the ghastly man sitting so close to him. He generally couldn't care less what people look like whoever they were, but in Grisaldo's case he was prepared to make an exception as he suddenly perceived that the man was actually quite ugly by any criteria, despite his full head of jet black wavy hair and athletic figure.

While of course he couldn't help what 'mother nature' had given him, Grisaldo was nevertheless in a position to smile occasionally and adopt a kinder facial disposition should he wish to do so. Paul became convinced that the man's disappointment in himself and envy of others such as he, who appeared to have accomplished so much more in their chosen profession, had somehow found expression in his cruel hostility and obvious personal negativity, a deep resentment at his lot in life that had somehow, but perhaps inevitably, become obvious in the deeply etched lines in his face, including his permanently downturned mouth. Paul might have forgiven him some of his malefactions if the man was kind to patients and junior staff, but he was neither. While the first of these was inexcusable, the second was predictable. Having acknowledged the malign nature of the man, Paul was fair to a fault and accepted that Grisaldo knew his business well and invariably made the correct and appropriate clinical decisions. In a way that made his strained relationship with him even more problematic than it already was. Even more distressing was his obvious ability to coerce people, especially junior doctors, to act in a way that was not natural to them. This was brought home to Paul in a particularly stark way when he learned that Grisaldo and his other, slightly less unpleasant accuser Marvin Cruvelier, whom he also despised though rather less so, were helped in their malicious rumour mongering by one of his most favoured and able junior oncologists. The evidence shown to him by his closer colleagues for this most upsetting collusion was unequivocal, but he wisely decided to say and do nothing about it.

However, he has a long memory and in the future he decided that while he would continue to be his usual charming self in his interactions with that younger colleague, nevertheless he resolved to do nothing whatsoever to help him in his future career. But neither would he do anything to hinder him. He is better than that, or at least he was at that particular time.

Medicine really doesn't need such a pathetic bunch of human snakes in the grass. They all knew what they did and why.

*

Despite the physical closeness of such intense personal negativity, Paul was a professional to a fault in his workplace and quickly got down to the very necessary business of both listening and cerebrating carefully. The first presentation was about a young woman with paroxysmal sensory symptoms in the right arm and leg, sometimes hundreds of times in one hour. From the depths of his knowledge, experience, and instinct he just knew that this poor woman had a rare form of Multiple Sclerosis. He resisted the temptation to volunteer the diagnosis to the assembled multitude but did ask a number of highly pertinent questions. The discussion about her case went on for what seemed to him to be an eternity, and no-one seemed to come up with a definite diagnosis. In the end he just couldn't restrain himself and decided to put everyone out of their misery and gave what turned out to be the correct diagnosis, one which was fully supported and confirmed by the radiological and other investigations. While one of his favoured junior colleagues gave him a friendly and knowing smile, he was able to discern a distinct scowl from Grisaldo who smiled and raised his heavy eyebrows as he looked in a conspiratorial way at his partner in crime Cruvelier. How his correct and insightful diagnosis must have irritated them. The second case was slightly more complex, but Paul realised the diagnosis very quickly. It was a young man suffering from AIDS who developed a bad headache and a variety of limb symptoms and weight loss. As soon as his brain MRI was flashed on the large screen in front of them, Paul twigged that the patient probably had a lymphoma which is a form of cancer, right up his street you might say. He immediately raised his hand and gave the diagnosis which turned out to be correct as the autopsy tissue analysis showed the classical features of a lymphoma. So as usual it was a full house for Paul. He could only imagine how his diagnostic perspicacity must annoy some of the less friendly and generous members of staff, and interestingly the greatest and friendliest comments to him were made by the neurologists and cardiologists, not to mention two of the ear, nose, and throat specialists whom he only knew through patient referrals and not personally. Grisaldo and Cruvelier probably loathed him even more than before, assuming such a thing was even possible. One of the nicest compliments came from a completely unexpected source, Mr Gerard Belmont-Smith, the aristocratic and elegant NHS head of the hospital's troubled but eminent Cardiothoracic Unit.

'Jolly good show, Professor,' the patrician surgeon

said to him in a profoundly genuine and friendly manner. Paul wondered why his own unit didn't contain such decent and splendidly eccentric consultants. But one must never be envious of those things that one does not have, in the same way that one never quite knows what one has until there is a real danger of losing it.

*

After an hour that seemed to pass very quickly, the meeting was disbanded and then everyone went their separate ways, some to their early afternoon ward rounds, some, such as Cruvelier, to see their private patients in another hospital, some to do some patient dictation and some, such as Paul, to consume lunch, in his case a frugal one of a simple sandwich and black coffee. As he munched away in his rather small hospital office, he felt a curious sense of both belonging to a peer group and yet not belonging and being a loner, though clearly a rather gifted one. While he should have felt a good deal of satisfaction, he did not do so, and only sensed an inexplicable feeling of personal alienation. He allowed himself to dissociate from his professional role for just a few minutes while he ate, his thoughts roaming through everything he considered interesting. All those thoughts abounded freely but the subject of medicine was absolutely nowhere. Rather like Paul.

*

After he had finished work for the day, insomuch as a man in his position can ever be truly finished in his work, he emerged from the yellow concrete-covered elevator into the massive multilevel hospital car park where he soon identified his own maroon automatic Mercedes. He rather liked his toys, both small and large, and he had always agreed with the notion that no-one is ever a hypocrite in their pleasures. That was one of his few concessions to what many would regard as normality. While he still has the insight to realise that he is perilously near the edge of a slow descent into madness, nevertheless he makes every attempt possible to keep a firm grip on the everyday routine of life, and to the external world he continues to be the epitome of a highly successful medical professional. How wrong can people be?

There are only two realities that Paul is aware of. One is himself and the other is the world around him. When he leaves the hospital, unless he is contacted at home by a distressed junior colleague about a particularly sick patient, he leaves that part of the world that comprises medicine behind. He then re-enters the non-medical world and emerges into the enclosed personal enclave that he calls family and home. At home he feels free to be as insane as he wants since no-one who can hurt him has the power to change his behaviour or influence him in any way. His wife Jane is fully aware of his extreme mental fragility and has decided to do nothing at this stage other than being as supportive as possible. Though she is so familiar with Paul's character and abilities and has the greatest of respect for his professional persona and work, nevertheless she is a keen observer of human behaviour and realises that her sweet-natured but severely troubled husband of twenty-one years could easily sink into the abyss of severe mental illness at any time in the near future. Later on, she may have no choice but to act in some way. That very thought terrifies her beyond description.

Later that evening Paul decides to take a leisurely stroll along the quiet and narrow streets in his upmarket neighbourhood of London's Highgate. It is 8.30 in the evening and since it is mid-summer there is still plenty of light in the sky above and he tries hard to make some kind of sense of the day. But soon the light will fade, even at this latitude, and the soulless artificial streetlamps will suddenly blink into action. Unfortunately for him he finds positive thinking impossible, and he has real difficulty in ascribing anything meaningful to what has become for him a rather boring and uneventful existence. For sure he is still sensible and aware enough of the value of people's lives and all the benefit they derive from his medical expertise and usually, but not always, effective treatment. After all, he knows he can't be of much help to everyone with cancer. No-one can. That springs from the cruel nature of malignant disease. He is not that dissociated from his work, but he still finds his daily existence largely devoid of meaning. At the grand round he certainly shone and was appreciated by many, but not all, of his so-called colleagues. For a moment he felt like an integral part of a close-knit group of doctors who had as a whole a very special knowledge of the inner workings of their fellow human beings, and was enthused, just as he once was in his youth, with the sheer thrill of knowing that as a member of an elite group he was actually doing something good for the world. While he still retains a vague memory of that young idealistic notion, he no longer believes it to be true, and his sense of medical community has long since evaporated into a void of cynicism. As a scientist he believes in absolute truth. As a doctor he believes in what works best. He really ought to be grateful for what he has in life – a noble profession, a fine family with a caring and intelligent wife and two fine teenage children, good health, and an expensive detached house to die for. But such reasonable gratitude takes no account of the inevitable irrationality of human beings, and Paul is no exception. So, what exactly is his problem? The problem is that while he knows he has a problem, he doesn't actually know what that problem is. What is still clear to his troubled soul is that there has been a definite and absolute dissociation between his professional role in life and his individual psyche. While in most cases that can be a healthy state of affairs, in Paul's case it presages only bad things in the future. It is less a loss of confidence than an alarming loss of the notion of self. But for the time being he can just about carry on with his personal identification. He must hold onto that somehow. It will be difficult, but it needs to be retained to maintain his grip on life, if not his very sanity.

CHAPTER 4

A TEST OF COMPASSION

It is 11 o'clock in the morning in Paul's new outpatient clinic and he has already seen four patients, all of whom have early-stage cancer of one kind or another. Using his vast experience and masterly expertise, he has been as positive as he possibly can in every case and formulated tentative treatment plans for all of them. He feels sorry for them all in a kind of professional way, and so far so good. The clinic has gone well, at least until the present time. Then he experiences a type of encounter that all doctors have to deal with infrequently during their careers, and it is an absolute requirement in such situations that they should keep their cool, maintain a professional manner at all times, and show the patient's family members as much courtesy as they can possibly muster under the admittedly difficult conditions. That is easier said than done of course.

He knew that trouble was on the way from the very first instance. The patient, a quiet but rather charming young man of twenty-two years called Peter with a probable lymphoma which is a cancer of the lymphatic system, was certainly not the problem. After all, treating lymphomas was a particular expertise of Paul's and he has conducted a good deal of research into these malignancies and was extremely good and experienced at dealing with them. But when the patient's father entered the consulting room soon after his son and glared at Paul with an extremely menacing look, he saw that the consultation was not going to be an easy one. Far from it, but all the same he must stay calm. The father made a kind of grunting noise as he sneered to the world and grabbed the nearest of the three available wooden chairs which he turned towards himself and sat in rather awkwardly with his short legs stretched out aggressively in front of him in the direction of Paul. The latter also sat down in his own uncomfortable wooden chair soon after he had politely introduced himself to both of them, shook hands with the young patient who also sat down slowly, and made an unsuccessful attempt to shake the father's hand who declined to extend his own hand to meet Paul's. Clearly this was going to be very difficult, if not rather dangerous.

The father fixed his eyes on Paul and started to speak before anyone else could.

'Let's get one thing clear, Professor Sellner-Smith, or whatever your posh double-barrelled name is, we've come here to you to get answers.'

'Yes of course,' said Paul.

'What's more,' the man went on, 'I'm not leaving this room until I get them, and you'd better deliver.'

This took Paul aback somewhat, but he was politeness itself.

'Well, I'll certainly do my very best for Peter and you as well of course.'

'Well, you'd better … or else there'll be trouble for you, I can assure you of that.'

'I see,' Paul replied as he experienced an almost painful frisson of intense dislike of this exceedingly rude and aggressive man. In fact, he didn't see at all. He just fumed internally.

'Oh do you? Good. I'm pleased we understand each other.'

Paul tried hard to give the man the benefit of the doubt and so was willing in his mind to attribute the father's extreme hostility to a deep sense of fear, possibly complicated by anxiety and depression. He had seen this kind of thing before and was professional enough not to rush to judgement, difficult as that might be to accomplish, especially when he's being verbally abused.

At this point young Peter looked at his father and tried to calm him down.

'Please dad,' he said, 'the Professor is going to do his best, and this ranting of yours isn't helping me or anyone else.'

Paul was glad to hear this but said nothing in response. He just waited instead.

Somehow Peter's words had a certain calming effect on his belligerent father and the consultation could therefore begin in earnest. While just thirty minutes had been allotted to deal with Peter's illness, these tense proceedings took a total of one hour and ten minutes, much of which was taken up with Paul's dealing with a raft of questions that the father fired at him in relentless and quick succession. But Paul is an expert, a veritable master of his medical sub-specialty trade and had no difficulty in dealing with the queries. His difficulty was, by contrast, in dealing with his emotions. But in such cases his long medical experience and training came to the rescue and ensured that he at least was able to keep himself on the rails so to speak.

What had clearly emerged from the long time he spent with them is that the diagnosis in Peter's case had been somewhat delayed, largely because his initial symptoms of tiredness and lassitude had been so general and non-specific. This meant that his kindly family doctor had carried out a few blood tests which, perhaps rather surprisingly, had shown nothing particularly untoward. So, there was a delay until his symptoms progressed and he had then noticed some lumps in his body where there should have been none. He was urgently referred to a general physician who was sufficiently alarmed to carry out further tests which were more worrying. Arrangements were made to take a biopsy (piece) of one of the swellings to try to get a tissue diagnosis but for some unexplained reason there was an administrative glitch, so the minor operation was delayed. Eventually everything was sorted out, the diagnosis was a lymphoma and that is how he eventually arrived in Paul's consulting room so he, the eminent Professor of Oncology (Cancer Studies), could deal with the illness once and for all. It turned out that either Peter's father had failed to understand what had been explained to him by the general physician or else the explanation given to him was just inadequate or even poor. Paul did not know which, if either, of these possibilities was true, but for whatever reason this delay and lack of effective communication was the underlying reason for the father's extreme hostility to all members of the medical profession whom he clearly regarded collectively as a 'bunch of incompetent quacks' to use his term of abuse.

Paul's profoundly detailed explanation of Peter's diagnosis and proposed future treatment was so clear and frank that eventually the father calmed down somewhat so that by the time they had finished he grudgingly accepted that he and his son had indeed finally ended up in the right department and under the right doctor (but he could not say the 'best' doctor for his illness). To Paul's amazement both Peter and his father shook his hand at the end of the consultation, and he even detected a faint smile form itself on the father's intensely sour face as they both exited the room. But there were no thanks from the father though there was fulsome thanks and praise from Peter. Well, that was a difficult job well done for sure. He duly arranged for Peter's early admission to one of his oncology beds to start his cycles of chemotherapy. This was done with his usual attention to detail and precision. But Paul needed a few minutes to recover from this rather bruising episode until he ushered in his final patient of the day, a young woman with advanced breast cancer. As he shook her hand and introduced himself to her, he gave her his profuse apologies for keeping her waiting for so long. At this she brushed aside his apologies, told Paul how delighted she was to meet him and over the course of just a few minutes she somehow managed to largely restore his faith in the dignity and kindness of human nature. That's just what he needed at that time.

*

He paid for his calmness under extreme provocation later that evening at home. Or, more accurately, both he and Jane paid the price for what had happened that morning. He managed to hold back his accumulated anger and frustration for the whole of dinner but soon after they had finished eating, a gathering storm cloud arose from within his consciousness, and there was very little that he could do to stop it from exploding into a damaging downpour. He recalls as a child having intermittent fits of temper tantrums at perceived injustices that were largely ignored by his parents, so there was already a worrying propensity to anger lurking in his background. But nothing could have prepared his wife for what she was about to witness.

Paul felt an indescribable feeling of rage rising up through his body and terminating as a painful and unbearable irritation in his head. It was so severe that in a curious way it was almost pleasurable, a feeling that he occasionally experienced when confronted by unreasonable patients or their relatives. It was rather like the increasingly recognised autonomous sensory meridian response (ASMR), but in reverse. How strange it is that pain and pleasure can be so closely related, a notion that had been described many years in the past by the great Plato writing in *The Apology* which recounted the execution of the philosopher Socrates by drinking the lethal poison hemlock. Paul slowly made his way up the house stairway to his small but heavily book-lined study which served as his private sanctum where he would write his scientific papers and spend a great deal of time thinking.

Sometimes he has a tendency to think too much to the extent that he can even become confused by the labour of his own thinking, something of which he was once accused by one of his old schoolteachers. But frankly he doesn't think much of such typically lordly pronouncements despite his respect for such teachers and the realisation of their exceptional importance in their pupils' development. For the record, he despised that particular teacher who even in retrospect was an opinionated idiot. That would actually be an accurate description of several of his colleagues.

As he sat back in his comfortable upholstered swivel chair, his gaze became fixed on the bottom row of historical medical books which adorned two of the study's high walls. He reckoned medicine had not changed greatly over the previous century, a view that would certainly not be held by most of his clinical brethren, or even by himself just a few days previously. Nothing was certain any more in his mind. It reminded him of life just six years before during the tumultuous coronavirus pandemic when life became very dystopian and uncertain for over two years, during which the government of the day and the so-called scientific experts made so many appalling mistakes that the good reputations of very few of them were able to survive the inevitable enquiry that followed the pandemic's eventual end. He literally shuddered when he thought of that terrible period during which the suicide rate skyrocketed and there were more deaths as a sad consequence of the prolonged and ineffective lockdowns than were apparently prevented by these severe, if not draconian, restrictions of people's natural freedoms.

As his mind wandered aimlessly among these painful past memories, he again became aware of a sudden rush of anger which this time he was powerless to suppress, something that had never happened to him before in such an unexpected manner. The inexplicable feeling seemed to begin in his legs and then rapidly ascend through his spine to finally infiltrate his brain. His first compulsion was to deface and trash all of his historical medical books, but somehow his love for these antique jewels of knowledge just managed to overcome his violent intent. But he was compelled to dissipate his rage. What he didn't know or understand (the two are not the same) was the underlying reason for his bizarre behaviour though he suspected it must have had something to do with how he'd been treated in his cancer clinic. What then ensued had always been a constant worry in recent times for Jane.

He opened the small bottle of permanent blue ink and poured all its contents over the many papers lying on his desk, including some key work documents of considerable importance. But that was just the beginning. He picked up the now empty bottle and threw it hard against the study window, producing a spray of numerous tiny glass fragments and a small linear crack in the window. Then he got hold of the metal desk lamp, yanked it free of the restraining electrical socket and hurled it against the lower part of one of the bookcases, producing no damage whatsoever except perhaps to the lamp's operation. Not satisfied with this display of senseless violence, he grabbed two of his most prized certificates of twenty years duration hanging proudly in gold frames on the study's back wall, and smashed them against the desk, again shattering the glass inside them, following which he tore the beautifully constructed documents into multiple shreds. In a final paroxysm of inexplicable but ferocious anger he seized the small but elegantly presented wedding photo of Jane and himself taken twenty-one years previously and threw it with great force against the right side wall of the study, an action that resulted in the breakage of the exquisitely carved wooden frame, following which he tore the charming and life-affirming photograph into small and tragic little pieces. Exhausted by this remarkable show of violence, he then sat down forlornly in his swivel chair, put his head in his hand, and cursed the very existence of the entire world. As can be imagined, that curse also included himself. Jane witnessed this carnage in silence.

CHAPTER 5

THE FLAIR THAT IS ASSUMED

Just about everyone in his hospital, as well as other national and international colleagues in his specialty, have the highest opinion of Paul. Unfortunately, that high opinion is not shared by Paul himself. This is not due primarily to modesty, false or otherwise, or humility (which are two entirely different qualities), but a consequence of his genuine opinion that he just isn't as good at his job in either medicine or science as other people seem to think. He is actually wrong on both counts, but that is his problem, and nothing will convince him otherwise. It is all part of his skewed perception of what is, and is not, work of high quality. Whenever he does something very well or is particularly successful then he usually regards this as due to luck or a fluke. But he will, however, accept that he is an intrinsically honest and principled man though he also knows that in recent times his hold on reality has been rather less than robust. Rather surprisingly, he has little insight into why this is the case. It is certainly not a matter of loss of self-confidence since he never had very much of that in the first place.

Just three days after his bruising encounter with the ultra-aggressive father of the young man with a lymphoma, Paul was walking briskly in the direction of his research laboratory in the North wing of the hospital when he was buttonholed by one of the three respiratory consultants. This specialist, Dr Edwina Pocock, was a woman of very considerable ability and experience for whom he had a great deal of personal and professional respect.

Accordingly, he temporarily abandoned his immediate plans and dropped everything for them to sit down on the nearest corridor chairs so he could give her his complete and undivided attention.

'I'm pretty sure this poor man is ending up in your territory, Paul,' she started. Paul gave her one of his friendly smiles before he replied.

'Well, Edwina, if you think so, then I'm sure you're right.'

'I think I am, Paul, and frankly I just wish I was

wrong about this. But, unfortunately, I'm not.'

'Well, I have to say that doesn't come as a complete surprise to me.'

Edwina smiled back ruefully and showed him the thin file of notes that she had been carrying under her right arm.

'You're very kind, Paul, as usual, but this man hasn't been dealt any kindness by life, that's for sure.'

Paul looked serious as he took the notes that Edwina had gently passed into his hands. 'OK, so what's the story here?'

Following this brief exchange, Edwina spent the next five minutes giving Paul a precise account of the patient's case. In brief, he was a forty-eight-year-old man who had until very recently been working as a carpenter, a trade that involves a high degree of practical skill. He had been smoking about thirty cigarettes a day ever since he was nineteen. He had recently noticed that his usual smoker's cough was worse, he'd lost over a stone in weight in the previous two months and he felt generally ill with no appetite. A chest X-Ray and then more detailed chest radiology had shown a highly suspicious mass in his left chest that could only be a lung tumour, probably malignant. Even more worrying was that there was definite evidence of metastatic spread as a bone scan and also CT scans of the abdomen and pelvis showed some suspicious bony lesions that greatly concerned her. A liver scan also showed two very suspicious areas of infiltration. All in all, this was not a good story and one that was likely to end badly.

After hearing the story of the man, whose name was Mark J Pressington, Paul closed the file and handed it back to Edwina, a distinct look of sadness etched on his handsome face.

'I think the situation is pretty clear from all this.'

'Yes,' Edwina replied, 'that's very much what I thought … but presumably we would also need a tissue diagnosis before a treatment plan can be started.'

'Yes, that's absolutely right,' replied Paul, 'we can arrange to admit him to our unit to do that, and also we need to do some more investigations, maybe a few more to be absolutely certain that the cancer has spread, and also where to, which I am sure it has from all the evidence so far.'

'I guess if that were the case then you'd be looking at chemotherapy with maybe radiation therapy?'

'Yes probably,' Paul replied. 'I don't think surgery is at all advisable here. But we may well put him on to a clinical trial we just started in these patients with advanced lung cancer …'

'A clinical trial?'

'Yes, assuming he gives informed consent, I think Mark may well qualify for entry into the trial where we're investigating the effect of combination therapy including a really promising new growth factor inhibitor.'

Edwina was clearly impressed.

'Well that sounds good. Maybe there's just a little bit of hope for this unfortunate man who also by the way is married with three teenage children.'

Paul gave a sympathetic groan, one often seen in medical doctors.

'That really is awful. Anyway, there's always hope for everyone, however sick they are. Every single patient is different, and also, in my experience, such as it is, it's usually been the case that sick patients with cancer who go into clinical trials often do better than one would normally have expected'.

'Well, I really hope that happens for Mark.'

'I have a strange feeling it just might'.

*

Paul is one of those people who always likes to get

things done and dusted straight away. He just hates to delay anything he's entrusted to do. The reason for this is not entirely clear, but it probably has more to do with his dislike of accumulated jobs on his 'to do' list rather than an intrinsic dynamism or natural aversion to laziness. Whatever the underlying motivation, the end result speaks volumes for Paul's efficiency and solid reputation as a highly reliable, conscientious, and through clinician. Notwithstanding this fine regard, he himself attributes his general efficiency to fear and potential stress and aggravation rather than anything more positive. That is so characteristic of this complex man.

So it was typical of him that he put off his research meeting for two hours and immediately made his way to the medical respiratory ward in the West wing of the hospital where this unfortunate individual with lung cancer was waiting patiently for his visit. Paul spent an hour with the man whom he thought was remarkably stoical about his diagnosis which the respiratory team had already explained to him. His longstanding smoking habit was almost certainly relevant to his disease. After he'd spoken with him very gently and gave him a cursory examination, he sat down with Mark and described to him the diagnosis and his intended treatment plan. He was pretty sure that he would be eligible for his new trial and that knowledge in itself gave some palpable hope to the patient. Paul thought the long-term prognosis was not at all good, but he still managed to strike a hopeful and positive note which seemed to satisfy Mark, at least for the present. He'd already had many tests but there were still several of them to do, including a more detailed assessment of the lung lesion with advanced radiography and also possibly a PET (positron emission tomography) scan to try to identify any lurking secondary deposits in Mark's body that may have been missed by these other investigations, and which could also provide him with a baseline assessment for the clinical trial. Overall, Paul had done his usual excellent job on the patient and had already established a friendly and honest rapport with him. Everyone was pleased, if not delighted, at the speed and quality of his consultation, and he had yet again demonstrated his clinical acumen and expertise to his patient, colleagues, and students. Everyone was impressed, apart, of course, from Paul. Now that is hardly a surprise. Someone had to pay for his success.

*

It is generally thought that the presence of suicidal ideation in people over the age of sixty-five years is form of medical emergency since so many of these unfortunate souls do actually go on to kill themselves. While Paul is only forty-nine years old, he doesn't fall into that high -risk age category, but all the same his thoughts away from work soon became dominated by a desire to exit the world and spare himself the inevitable emotional suffering and frustration that he knows for sure he's more than likely to face in the future. His future, that is. He would never try to speak for the emotional turmoil of others. For all he knows some of his clinical colleagues may feel the same as he does. But somehow Paul doesn't think that is at all likely. He can only feel for himself. Having temporarily discarded the role as a leading medical doctor when away from the hospital, he was now in serious danger of losing his private role as a family man. Few things in life can be more dangerous than that.

When he arrived home in Highgate around six o'clock in the early evening after dealing so well with the poor man with lung cancer, he seemed remarkably normal, even philosophical, to his wife Jane and probably also to his two small children as far as they could assess anything at all in the human psyche. He interacted perfectly normally with little Charlotte and Gavin, and indeed an external observer would perceive nothing amiss in his behaviour and general demeanour. But the fact that Paul was acting more normally than he'd ever done in the previous six months was enough to send warning signs to Jane who knew his rather quirky character better than anyone else alive. Within two hours it was clear that her concern and impending sense of doom was fully justified. It was a classic example of the calm preceding the gathering storm.

At eight o'clock that evening he walked out of his front door in short sleeves as it was still balmy and very warm, a tranquil end to a splendid mid-summer's day. As he walked rather aimlessly along the still busy but quite narrow streets in his upmarket neighbourhood, his mind began to race as a barrage of images and haphazard thoughts suddenly infiltrated his consciousness with a violence that greatly surprised him. Perhaps he was more disturbed by recent events than he'd initially thought. After he'd walked absent minded for about an hour, something seemed to click inside his head. At first, he was quite frightened as it was a novel and unusual, if not somewhat frightening, feeling that he hoped was not an indication of an impending stroke. He realised this was unlikely on purely statistical grounds, but there was nothing about being relatively young and in good health that guaranteed immunity from a bodily catastrophe like a brain haemorrhage. Paul had been a doctor for long enough to know that even the apparently healthiest people can be suddenly struck down with a debilitating illness that can change their life forever. Interestingly, he was far more frightened by the idea of being permanently disabled than facing sudden extinction from some lethal bodily episode. Perhaps it was that notion of a sudden and painless death that was a key driver of what happened to him next.

He remembered surprisingly little of the events that followed soon afterwards and perhaps that was just as well. Several cars and as well as a few large lorries sped along the main road that he was walking along while he began to be aware of an odd tingling sensation at the back of his head, a feeling that seemed strangely familiar. It seemed so simple to Paul at that particular moment. He was absolutely sure he wanted his life to end and here was an ideal opportunity to achieve that in just a few seconds. He decided to suddenly walk in front of an oncoming lorry and terminate his miserable existence on the cruel and unjust planet. He did not fear pain or injury and just wanted to do the deed and then have done with it. As a long and very large lorry sped along the main road towards him on his side, Paul prepared to jump directly in front of it and be killed instantaneously. That there could be no other outcome, he was absolutely certain. It was important not to give any indication to the oncoming driver or to be half-hearted in the act's execution. He must be unswerving in his insanity. Yet he had no sense of terror, only one of inevitability. But just as he was about to jump onto the road to irreversible extinction, two new thoughts struck him in quick succession and just managed to stay his hand. He still maintained enough insight and sanity to realise that in perpetrating this suicidal act he would almost certainly be condemning the lorry driver to a life of regret and recurrent nightmares, not to mention prolonged legal agony. Also, he thought of his two young children who would not understand his motivation and would likely never recover from the suicide of their father who they would probably miss for the rest of their lives. He may be totally embittered and irrational, but they were still far too young to have the faintest notion of what was driving him to this final and brutal act of self-destruction. Because of this temporary surge of rational thought, Paul stepped back and decided to live, at least for a little while yet. It was one thing to destroy himself but quite another to destroy forever the lives of three other people. He should also have thought of his understanding wife Jane, but he did not. That fact in itself surely indicated the sheer extent of his mental anguish.

CHAPTER 6

THE SECRETS OF THE LABORATORY

As Paul entered the vast lecture hall, magisterial in its symmetrical architecture, he experienced an oddly familiar combination of excitement and familiarity. How many times during his already distinguished career had he been exposed to endless presentations on his specialty subject, most of them quite mundane if not frankly boring, most very well performed and presented, and just a few of them truly interesting and important? The one thing he always tried to be was interesting when presenting his research work, whether it was for the benefit of students or else his scientific and medical peers at local meetings or at prestigious international symposia like the current one that he'd been generously invited to attend. An old scientific boss of his always used to advise him to tell a good story and not bombard people with endless data, most of which would never filter through into any listener's consciousness anyway, no matter how hard they tried. That was good advice for sure but presenting complex ideas and research data in an interesting and coherent way was never that easy, but it was still vital not to bury important findings in a mass of well-nigh incomprehensible facts and figures. Why do so many people always make that mistake?

Have they no insight? He always understood far more from a careful reading of a scientific paper than from an oral presentation of the same findings no matter how clear and compelling the speaker might be. Paul knew of course that there were some people who had the ability to extract all that really mattered from a speaker's slides, but unfortunately he was not one of them. This failing, or at least that was how he interpreted it, was just one of his apparent shortcomings as a clinical scientist that Paul saw in himself and perhaps underlay his increasing sense of personal failure and lack of confidence both in himself and what he always produced in publications on a regular basis. The only thing that he was truly certain about was his scientific honesty and total integrity. These were outstanding qualities that everyone else recognised with no small degree of admiration, but to Paul it was just obvious that he should act in this manner, and he never saw them as worthy of any particular praise. If only he knew how many people actually carry out their business. The tragedy here is that Paul has now become oblivious to other people and the outside world, which to him represents a constant threat to both his work and his very existence. How wrong can you be? In Paul's case everything normal around him had become something to be wary of.

The truth of it is that he found almost everything he heard in the oral presentations, and also viewed on the supporting posters in the evenings, completely boring, unimportant, and mechanical. There was scientific fluency present for sure, no question about that, but he perceived nothing in them that was truly new or innovative. This was not that unusual at such meetings, but he had travelled a long way to attend this one which was being held in San Diego in the West Coast of the United States, and he was very disappointed. Perhaps some new paradigm shift in his oncology field would suddenly emerge in the following year, one that could be rapidly transferred to the clinic for the benefit of his patients, some of whom were even then enduring hideous suffering from their cancer. These observations of his lent considerable weight to his long-held belief that the greatest advantage of these huge meetings was to meet and interact with his international scientific peers, many of whom were present and, he was pretty sure, would have a similar view of the conference as him. It is often at such meetings that serious and novel ideas are spawned between the different delegates, and quite frequently new collaborative projects can be established, leading to exciting discoveries at best and an enrichment of the scientific community at worst even if nothing productive comes out of it. He tells himself that he must keep positive in the presence of so much enthusiasm and talent, especially evident in the more junior delegates who seemed to Paul as if they were literally bursting with energy, enthusiasm, and commitment. He was once just like them before life inevitably turned him into an inveterate cynic.

On the second day of the conference, he was scheduled to give his keynote lecture at a plenary session with perhaps two thousand interested and not so interested souls in the audience. He had prepared this with his trademark attention to detail, and even at his senior level, he had taken the precaution of first practising it to himself. He was mildly anxious, but after much experience of giving major talks, he had long since lost his previous terror at the very thought of speaking in front of a large audience. He had some very interesting findings from his own laboratory to present that he knew would excite at least some of the people there. But he did not reveal everything that his research group had discovered as he was mildly concerned that some unscrupulous scientist might steal his ideas. That had happened to him just once before, so he was always very guarded about what he divulged to even quite close colleagues. After what many experts and non-experts thought was a masterly performance, he completed his twenty-five-minute talk with the usual generous acknowledgements to the youngsters who had actually performed the work and his various national and international collaborators. He received a warm reception with nods and smiles in every corner which was a big relief to him. Clear and enthusiastic as he may have appeared to the external world, Paul found the whole experience both stressful and rather boring, but he had no difficulty whatsoever in fielding the several questions, a few penetrating in nature, that followed his talk. Job done.

Later that evening at the poster session, accompanied by a remarkably generous distribution of soft drinks, wine, and assorted buffets which to

Paul seemed more like a feast, he was buttonholed by an old colleague from Sweden. His name was Lars Vesalius and he was a distinguished cancer scientist with whom he'd collaborated on a project ten years previously. Lars was of a similar age to Paul, and like him was tall and handsome but had a full head of wavy blonde hair in contrast to Paul's which was dark brown. Lars was also more thickset in build than Paul who was as lean as a whippet. A further difference was that while Lars had a permanent smile on his lips, Paul usually greeted the world with a disdainful scowl.

After greeting each other warmly and shaking hands, Lars smiled broadly and complimented Paul on his talk that afternoon.

'That was a superb talk you gave today, Paul,' he told him.

'Thanks. That's very kind of you, Lars. It seemed to go OK.'

'It was superb … you're just being your normal modest self, as always.'

Paul blushed slightly. He never had been good at taking compliments. This was less a matter of innate modesty than one of chronically low personal esteem.

'Well, Lars, some of us have a lot to be modest about.'

At this the Swedish specialist just smiled and then looked at his friend askance.

'Well anyway it was very good, whatever you think. Hey let's get some food. I just can't believe the opulence of this place. The amount of food is crazy.'

Paul concurred and nodded knowingly.

'Well, it might seem that way to we Europeans. Maybe we just don't know how to eat.'

'I think the English and the Scandinavians just eat in moderation and much more healthily.'

'Maybe… maybe. Perhaps that's why the Americans tend to be so big,' said Paul.

'And so clever – just look at all their Nobel Prize winners.' Paul looked straight into Lars' eyes.

'Well, you would certainly know about that, wouldn't you?'

Lars smiled ruefully at this and ushered his friend towards the nearest buffet table which was literally laden with an abundance of meats, breads, dips, and small sandwiches. One thing for sure was that no-one at this symposium would go home hungry.

*

One day after arriving back home, having endured stoically the uncomfortable overnight flight from sunny San Diego, Paul started to ruminate about his time away from London. He made a choice many years previously never to go business class unless he was lucky enough to be upgraded from economy by the airline, but this had only happened on two prior occasions. He would rather use his precious discretionary research funds for research work or to transport his juniors rather than his own private comfort. This was a practical and perfectly sensible decision, but again was evidence of just how insignificant he considered himself in the general scheme of things compared to other (less gifted as it happens) academics whom he erroneously considered to be his intellectual superiors. For a doctor with an excellent understanding of his patients, he was particularly poor at assessing the merits and demerits of many of his colleagues. That excludes, of course, the ones he hates with a vengeance, and there are several of those.

Paul was in what he felt was an unusual position in that he was both inside and outside the academic system. While he knew full well that he was a well-respected clinician-scientist with many important national and international contacts, nevertheless he was also convinced that he was the classical outsider. He viewed with some detachment the goings-on of one kind or another at the international conference he'd just attended and had nothing but contempt both for the (in his view|) unjustified self-importance and arrogance of some of his peers, and the pathetic obsequiousness and genuflecting that he observed in so many aspiring youngsters shown towards certain senior 'big shots' whom they purported to admire so much. What exactly are these people trying to achieve by doing this? But while Paul had an intense dislike of such pathetic individuals, this was as nothing when compared to his profound hatred of himself. He also made an observation which more than amused him. The observation was that there was a kind of inverse relation between a person's true distinction in their field, based on an objective appraisal of their life's accomplishments, and their level of observed humility shown towards other people no matter what their station in life. So, the more distinguished the individual is, whatever their specialty, then the more humble they tended to be. While that is obviously not always the case, it was a pretty common observation of his. It is the presumptuous high-level mediocrities in life that Paul most fears. He does not include himself in that ubiquitous yet contemptible group as he doesn't consider himself to be at a high level, but just a mediocrity. Wrong again. While some people are genuinely modest about their achievements, others show humility to others including ardent admirers. The modest person genuinely thinks they are nothing special and that anyone in the right place could do what they have done, while the humble person knows full well the great extent of his or her true worth in their field but has the personal integrity, kindness, and good grace to make little of their massive achievements in the presence of others. In Paul's case, he was certainly modest in this sense but was not humble because he felt he had nothing to be humble about. As had once before been said about him, he can sometimes be confused by the sheer labour of his own thought processes. Well, at least he was capable of thinking, however perverse and erroneous that process may be. Unfortunately, this obvious realisation was of little comfort to him.

*

The following day was the start of the weekend so he should have been more relaxed in the more tranquil surroundings of his Highgate home than he actually was. The paradox of his life at this progressively low point was that, despite his bizarre mental state, he was perfectly able to maintain a thoroughly convincing façade of normality at work while simultaneously displaying several signs of total irrationality at home. The extent to which he had insight into this strange behavioural dichotomy has never been clear to anyone, least of all to him. What was absolutely clear, however, is that his wife Jane had been increasingly concerned at her husband's mental state and was on the point of suggesting that Paul seek advice from another health professional, ideally an insightful and empathetic psychiatrist. While she did have someone in mind, a particularly kind and insightful middle-aged woman with a fine reputation, she also knew that Paul felt that everyone in his hospital was 'leaky' in that no personal details about staff could ever be kept confidential. If that really were the case amongst medical professionals, then it would represent a very sorry state of affairs. Surely all personal details of patients and doctors alike should always be kept entirely private and confidential? While she still has faith in the notion of patient confidentiality, she also has a fear that Paul may be right in his views. If so, then it would be yet another example of everything in the world just falling apart, just as it had almost done many years previously during the horrific coronavirus pandemic that was still talked about and discussed by experts in so many different fields even after six years since it ended worldwide.

After their usual evening meal, which was invariably excellent since, among her other sterling qualities, Jane was also a superb cook, Paul made his way upstairs to enter his private study and think hard about science and scientists. He had been greatly affected by all that he'd witnessed at the oncology symposium in the US. But the more he thought about the subject, the more confused and frustrated he became, mainly because he just couldn't be sure of anything. But, just as he realised that profound and intrinsic limitation, he had what might be thought of as an epiphany since that lack of certainty itself was both the problem and the point of all scientific activity. He was sure someone else in history must have come to the same conclusions and had similar, if not identical, insights. But he had arrived there from first principles, all fuelled no doubt by his abnormal mental state. It did not occur to him that his high intellect may also have played a role.

There was no certainty whatsoever in Paul's life except the two great certainties of death and the paying of income tax. He was wary and frightened of both. Even magisterial bedrocks of human knowledge are never certain, as in the case of Newton's theory of gravitation which steadfastly stood the test of time for over two hundred years until Einstein proved that it was itself not completely adequate to explain gravitation on a cosmic scale, and so superseded it as a universal truth. Even that great theory is likely to be refined by some future genius or critical observation of the Universe. For all Paul knows there may be multiple Universes and he may be living in just one of them. He reckons that if that theory of multiverses is true then he clearly got the raw deal because he feels life has not treated him well. In fact, life itself has not been treated well. All scientific experiments and explanations can do is give the best possible approximation to the truth, or, as Kant might say, 'the thing in itself'. These will inevitably be at least slightly wrong, and in due course further scientific experimentation will get us even nearer the actual truth of matter and the world. But all scientific efforts will try to refute existing dogma until we can derive the best possible approximation to what is really true in the world. Paul found this line of reasoning comforting since it gave him some relief from his constant questioning of both himself and everything around him. Unfortunately, this relative peace of mind did not last very long. To be exact, it lasted for forty minutes only. It will also not come as a surprise to anyone that he also an agnostic. He just can't be certain enough to be either a believer or an atheist.

He just doesn't know.

One thing he was sure of, however, was that he would be better off dead. That in the long run would be best for his wife and also for his two children though he was always wary of setting them both up for a long-term psychiatric complex of some kind. Nevertheless, that evening he felt a certain *frisson* of courage that he hadn't experienced before. It's called a delusional mood. Accordingly, almost as if his actions were being controlled by an external agent, he picked up an old Swiss Army penknife that he'd been given by his late father many years before and locked himself into the upstairs bathroom. He was able to do this since he had the door key that could lock it from both sides. Once inside he ran the bath for a few minutes until it was nearly full of hot water, undressed completely and then stepped in slowly. It was initially very hot on his skin but soon it was transformed into a delicious soft feeling which seemed to want him to doze off and sleep. He reached for his penknife with his right hand and opened the longer of the two sharp blades. He thought he would do it the Roman way and cut the main arteries in both wrists so that he would bleed to death painlessly in the warm water. But this was easier imagined than actually done. He made a few tentative nicks in his left wrist which were superficial though they still managed to draw a little blood. He then halted for a few seconds and the previous courage and desire to terminate his miserable existence forever quite suddenly deserted him. Or else he just might have had second thoughts about taking such drastic action. At that very moment he was aware of Jane banging on the bathroom door with her fist and crying out to him and asking him what on earth was going on.

'I'm fine, Jane,' he cried out as he lied outrageously to her.

'Good,' replied Jane, 'but why have you locked the door?'

'Oh, just to get a bit of privacy you know,' Paul replied, raising his voice slightly.

'Really? Paul, can you please tell me what's going on? I'm really scared now.'

'Oh, it's fine. I'll just come out and unlock the door in a second.'

Jane was still terrified at what he might do, or what he may already have done. 'Right, that's very good. Now, don't slip on the wet floor.'

Slowly Paul got out of the bath, hid the penknife in a cupboard below the marble sink, and unlocked the bathroom door.

'Thank God for that,' Jane said to him as she held him in a close embrace, 'you poor darling, but you seem absolutely OK.'

'Of course,' he said in a surprised tone, 'why wouldn't I be?'

Then she saw the thin trickle of blood running down his left wrist and forearm.

CHAPTER 7

THE APPOINTING COMMITTEE

There is always something rather exciting just before interviewing candidates for a major medical consultant position, and this probably springs from the uncertain outcome in most, but not all, cases. Paul was the senior University Oncology consultant on the appointments committee which had only recently been put together to choose a new Senior Lecturer in the department. However, he'd had enough previous experience of these committees to know that the eventual outcome was seldom a foregone conclusion, and, distinguished and well respected as he undoubtedly was, he could easily be outvoted by the other committee members who might well favour a different candidate than the one he might want. In the current situation there was undoubtedly a very strong field to choose from, though in Paul's view one individual among the five short-listed candidates stood out from the others in all aspects of achievement. But he privately admitted to his three fellow academics, all of whom told him they agreed with his very fair assessments, that he had a bad feeling that somehow she wouldn't be successful that afternoon. Unfortunately, Paul's 'bad feelings' usually turned out to be right.

The committee comprised the usual mix of medical and other academics, eight in all, with five men and three women. As well as the four University-employed oncologists, there were two NHS cancer specialists from Paul's department, and two other University Professors, one of whom was from the Chemistry department, and who was also a required senate assessor there to see fair play and the strict following of regulations, and the other a distinguished basic immunologist. The committee was chaired by a University Professor of Law to whom Paul took an instant dislike, a feeling driven at least in part by the fact that he'd woken up that morning with a splitting headache that seemed to be unresponsive to aspirin or paracetamol, thus making him particularly irritable. The proceedings started with each person giving a brief introduction to themselves, which they all did in a perfunctory manner. Paul was particularly brief and succinct, a performance which was immediately picked up by the unpleasant Chair who asked him in a remarkably rude manner to be speak more clearly and say more. Paul was so incensed by what he perceived as a gross impertinence that he gave a sharp retort to the rude legal expert.

'Are you naturally a rude person, Professor Loftinghouse, or do you actually work on your propensity to rudeness?' Paul then glared at the man in a very intimidating manner.

The hapless Professor of Law had probably never been spoken to like that by anyone in his life and was clearly pretty shocked at Paul's aggressive jibe. So, after a few shocked seconds, he wisely gave no reply and just got on with the process. Paul noticed at that point that several committee members had a slight smile on their lips as if they had rather enjoyed his sharp upbraiding of the pompous Chair. The latter then gave a verbal list of all five candidates and confirmed that everyone on the committee had received and read the various CVs, referees' letters, and the candidates personal letters and statements explaining why they were all the best thing since sliced bread and should be appointed to this plum position. Paul had seen it all before. In reality, any one of the five candidates – three men and two women, one of whom was from another University outside London and who, in Paul's opinion, had the greatest potential as a future oncology leader – would be perfectly acceptable to him and in reality they were spoiled for choice. But, like most extremely talented people, Paul could easily detect genuine talent and real potential in young up-and-coming doctors, and he was quite sure that the young woman from outside was the best person for the job. But it was also important to see how well they all acquitted themselves at interview as not everyone can withstand, or indeed shine at, such a formal ordeal of this kind.

The first candidate, a lecturer in his own department, gave a competent but rather boring interview and was clearly not going to be a leading contender. The woman of thirty-two years from the outside University gave an outstanding performance and was to Paul as impressive in reality as her outstanding CV. He also thought the hitherto very inbred department would benefit from an injection of a bit of diversity and external talent so that was also in her favour. The third candidate, a man who was a lecturer in another London Hospital, was a very competent doctor and academic but gave a disastrous interview and seemed to go completely to pieces under the pressure and scrutiny of the nine-person committee. Paul was very sorry to witness such a personal collapse and he felt deeply empathetic for the poor man. The fourth candidate, an accomplished man of thirty-four years, who was a senior research fellow in his own department, also gave a fine interview. Paul thought he would be perfectly acceptable to everyone, but he was not as impressive as the young woman he favoured.

Finally, around four o'clock in the afternoon they interviewed the fifth candidate who was an older woman from an outside London hospital, also gave a good interview but her CV was relatively weak in comparison to the others. But she showed much less fear of the committee than the four others and was more suave in her answers to questions than her counterparts.

When all five candidates had been interviewed, the Chair asked each individual member of the committee to rank them in order of quality and thereby indicate who they most wanted to be appointed. This process took about ten minutes following which Paul started to experience an unpleasant feeling in his abdomen. When it came to the actual vote there was a tie between Paul's favoured candidate and the fourth individual, the research fellow from his own department, each of whom received four votes.

'Oh dear,' murmured Paul quietly to his colleague on his left who gave him her most reassuring smile and a slight shrug of the shoulders. One of his own University colleagues voted for the man and the chemist voted for his favoured candidate. Since no-one would shift their position, it was now the Chair's prerogative to cast the deciding vote to break the deadlock, according to University regulations. He voted for the man. Paul could not decide at that moment whether this most unpleasant law Professor voted in this way in order to spite Paul, or else came to his decision as a result of his genuine and considered opinion. He would never know the answer to that question, but he always suspected it was the former consideration that dominated. Naturally, it never occurred to him that perhaps the answer was both of these as they are not mutually exclusive. Perhaps the Chair was not even sure himself.

As they poured out of the elegant room that had served as the interview venue, Paul was more philosophical and accepting of this outcome than his colleagues thought likely. He had seen it all before and it was very much as he had suspected. Perhaps they just wanted to appoint the devil they already knew and not risk exposure to an unknown quantity. If that were actually true, which he strongly suspected was the case, then it was a decision they would rue one day in the future as this talented young woman was going places for sure and fast. He decided he would write an encouraging personal handwritten note to her in the near future. It also reinforced his increasing belief that he himself was of little importance in the general scheme of things, and especially so in his own Institution. This episode only added to his increasing sense of failure and poor standing in real terms of the political power that he could weald for good. But life goes on and he would do his best to support the newly appointed candidate.

Paul had lost none of his sense of fairness and professional identity.

*

Paul had known for many years that life is unfair, and no-where is that obvious truth more evident than in the world of medicine. Time and time again he had seen how young doctors of talent had been denied the opportunity to shine because of some tribal prejudice that excludes outsiders, however gifted. Things had improved considerably in recent years, but he still valued talent and ability over professional preferment and even what he regarded as misguided virtue signalling. That very day he had seen a perfect example of what concerned him most. It was perhaps more a question of a collective failure of imagination rather than a limitation of good morals. He guessed that affairs had always operated like this.

Later that day, as he was trying to relax at home, in short sleeves that evening as it was still so unusually warm, he felt compelled to take a short spin in his recently purchased automatic Mercedes car because he wanted to take his mind off his nagging concerns and increasing confusion which were now causing him to doubt his own sanity. Thus, he had at least a little insight into his own psyche. After settling down in the car's comfortable upholstered driver's seat, he switched on the ignition and drove off slowly along the narrow road where he lived into the larger main road that he knew so well. The quiet rushing sound of the engine was soothing to his mind and increasingly he felt a deliciously cool sensation circulate throughout his body, making him relax increasingly as his vehicle gathered speed. Within a few minutes he found himself driving through still familiar territory as he left his immediate neighbourhood behind and sped along thinly populated but wide roads in the direction of London's inner core. Though it was midsummer, the light was now beginning to fade, and quite suddenly Paul became aware of a line of regularly spaced streetlamps becoming silently reborn as they lit up the strangely subfusc roads and pavements with their rather understated luminescence. As he drove along the near empty streets towards the city centre, he felt an increasing sense of mental and physical tranquillity that was new to him, and he wondered why he hadn't thought of doing this before.

After about ten minutes of steady driving, Paul became aware of a familiar tingling sensation at the back of his head. It was not at all unpleasant and he regarded it as a kind of old friend that presaged a period of calm meditation and relaxation even though he had to keep his eyes on the road ahead and also avoid any stray pedestrians who may not have seen his car approach them. But he soon noticed that his surroundings were somehow no longer familiar to him, and he felt increasingly lost even though he knew that he was driving through streets he'd passed through many thousands of times before. It was all known urban territory. This was a strange state of affairs to be sure, but curiously enough Paul felt little sense of distress. He should have done so as most people certainly would. It was interesting that though this spatial disorientation was manifest quite suddenly, nevertheless Paul's awareness of this change was gradual and stress-free into the bargain. It was almost like the effect of a 'pre-med' before a hospital operation where there is a definite dissociation between the fact of pain and its perception. When the anaesthetist inserts a large cannula into the patient's hand vein before being put to sleep and oblivion, there is a full awareness of its painful and unpleasant nature, yet it is not accompanied by the usual distress. The entire procedure becomes oddly objectified. Thank goodness for anaesthetics and their power to make one forget everything that may have happened.

As Paul basked dreamily in the strange reverie induced by the smooth progress of his Mercedes, he must have lost concentration momentarily, and over the course of no more than a few seconds his car smashed headlong into a tall lamppost on the left side of the wide road. The brief but loud thwacking noise this caused immediately jerked him out of his dreamlike state. He was uninjured but deeply shaken, but the car was a write-off. When he stepped out of the car and saw the shambles his lack of attention had caused, he was appropriately horrified. He immediately called the police who were in attendance within a few minutes which more than impressed him, and he also called Jane on his cell phone to let her know what had happened. To his surprise she sounded remarkably calm once it was clear to her that he was unharmed. In the event, the insurance company underwrote the very high cost of the wreck of a car, and he was fortunate not to have been prosecuted by the police. This may have been good luck, but he also suspected that his noble profession as a cancer specialist probably also helped more than a little. Well, he does deserve some luck after all he's been though.

CHAPTER 8

THE POWER OF THE MEDIA

There are two groups of people who truly frighten Paul. They are lawyers and journalists. Accordingly, he does everything he can to avoid both groups like the plague. While the former can ruin your profession, the latter can ruin your reputation.

In practice he's never had a significant problem with a lawyer, either as a patient, or as a patient's relative, but he still very wary of them all the same. In his experience, though, these legal people don't become particularly litigious when they become very ill as they soon realise they are just like everyone else. Nevertheless, they still know exactly how to sue you if the need arises. So, he is always on his guard. But he is afraid of journalists even more. He's had a couple of patients who were also journalists, and he hadn't had any problems with them, so far as he is aware.

But one never knows what they might write about their hospital experience, including their consultant's perceived expertise, at some future date, either in a newspaper or a book. So that's why he's always very wary with these clever people. Once an allegation of any kind appears in print then it is there forever and can be extremely difficult to refute if it's erroneous or, more likely, one-sided or exaggerated.

So, his anxiety can only be imagined when the powerful and persuasive Chief Executive of his hospital asked him to speak to a well-known medical journalist about the work of his Oncology department, including the nature of cancer, what are the current therapies available, and how the general prognosis of cancer has changed in recent times. The interview would take place in Paul's own office in the hospital, would likely last about an hour, and selected parts of it would appear on a television programme on cancer that would shortly be aired for the general public. In practice, of course, only about five minutes at most of Paul's interview would be used for the broadcast but that would be standard practice and besides, clearly he wouldn't be the only specialist to be interviewed. Paul had done two of these kind of interviews in the past, one for a popular newspaper which managed to get almost all of the details wrong (he suspects some of this was deliberate to make it more readable and interesting to the public), and one for a science programme that managed to get almost all the details right. So his past experience had been mixed. He was aware that a clever interviewer and camera operator could make the interviewee look rather stupid or pompous if they so wished but in this particular case proposed he knew the journalist by reputation and he seemed like a pretty solid reporter. So, perhaps against his better judgement, he agreed to do the interview. After all, he knew his subject inside out, from both the scientific and clinical angles, and he *was* meant to be one of the UK's leading cancer specialists, so if not him then who else? Also, someone else might give a very misleading account of affairs. At least he could be accurate and would make a decision to be very careful and guarded when responding to the more provocative or controversial questions that he would inevitably have to field. Also, he must remember to sit still in his chair and not swivel from side to side as an experienced television journalist once told him that doing that would make him look shifty, which is also a deliberate trap they sometimes set for evasive politicians whom they do not like.

The following morning, he took a taxi to the

hospital since he no longer had access to his car following his major accident, sat down in his comfortable swivel office chair, and tried hard to relax by practising deep breathing prior to the television interview scheduled for 10 o'clock in the morning. Though he is an undoubted expert in his field, he knows all too well that, especially in the prevailing ultra-politically correct atmosphere, just one careless phrase could be totally misinterpreted and land him in very hot water. His heightened anxiety was therefore entirely understandable. But he needn't have worried to this extent because the journalist, a man called Louis Eltringham, was a kind and considerate man of about forty years who managed to put Paul totally at ease, which was no mean feat given his very level of obvious worry. He told Paul before the interview what questions he intended to ask him. No problems were anticipated.

Louis and his camera operator were clearly true professionals and knew their jobs just as well as Paul knew his. He was struck by the brightness of the lights in his office shined straight at him for the interview, but his eyes soon adapted to the level of required illumination. Paul was also surprised to see such tiny cassettes being loaded into the main camera so clearly TV technology had advanced considerably over the previous few years. When he expressed, slightly jokingly, his fear that he would probably come over as yet another absurd looking expert, Louis, not jokingly at all, told him that in fact he was very photogenic and that he should have no worries whatsoever in that regard. Thus, reassured and flattered, Paul suggested that the proceedings should begin. The first twenty minutes went very well indeed. Paul was asked several simple questions to allow the lay public watching the programme to understand why cells become malignant in the first place. This Paul explained with his trademark clarity and everything he said could be easily understood by just about anyone in the target audience. So far, so good. The discussion then went on to the typical symptoms that a patient suffering from cancer might experience. Paul started very well as before but then quite suddenly, and without any warning, he became unable to find the right words for what he wanted to say. To the observer he started to talk intermittent gibberish, and the more Paul panicked at what had happened to him, then the worse his mangled speech became. After two minutes of this verbal agony, Louis halted the interview and asked Paul if he was feeling OK. Paul had a mild headache which he attributed to poor sleeping and the stress of the recent car crash, but he rapidly felt under control again, especially when the camera operator, a young man called Russell, gave him a glass of cold water to drink. Thus refreshed, Paul apologised to them both for what had just happened, which he assured them was just due to his great anxiety about the interview and signalled his willingness and desire to continue. This was duly done, and Paul had no further problems with his speech for the next hour or so. Apart from that early episode, which Louis kindly dismissed as just one of those things that often happen under these tense circumstances, everything had gone well, and Paul did a really good job of explaining the nature of cancer and what specialists like him can do about it. Louis also promised that he would discard the embarrassing few minutes of the interview. Paul trusted him and had no doubt whatsoever that the journalist would keep his word.

After thanking Louis and Russell for their time and consideration, the two men left to put together their programme, and Paul went back to his small hospital office so he could think about how the morning had gone and also what exactly had happened to him during the interview. He truly did not think there was any insidious cause of the incident and did everything he could in terms of being busy to dismiss it from his thoughts. So, he did some unfinished dictation on some of the patients he had seen recently, he read over a manuscript that one of his junior research workers had given to him for his comments, and he also glossed over some of the few articles that he could actually understand in that week's Nature journal. As far as he was concerned, it was just back to business as normal.

*

Jane had made a special meal for them both that evening, ostensibly to make Paul feel better after his car accident of two days previously. But the truth is that whatever she made would have been excellent since she was a naturally gifted cook though she tended to deny this for some obscure reason, probably related to her natural modesty. The meal of tender roast chicken, sweet potatoes and asparagus spears followed by apple charlotte and lemon ice cream went down extremely well, but when it was time for coffee and mint chocolates, they noticed that they had no milk to soften the taste of coffee. Paul complimented his wife on her usual superb cooking and decided to pay a brief visit to the local supermarket to buy some milk to make good the deficit. Accordingly, he walked briskly the half a mile to the nearest supermarket since he felt he could do with the walk and, besides, he had no choice since he had no car, and he couldn't be bothered to use his wife's small Ford focus. After entering the surprisingly large, high ceilinged supermarket, he made a quick beeline for the milk section and grabbed a litre bottle of their usual semi-skimmed milk. He was a man in a hurry, so he rushed back to the checkout queue and waited patiently for the woman in front of him to complete and pay for her purchases. That was when he lost control of his temper for the first time in his adult life.

It all happened in an instant and could have so easily been avoided. He was next in line to be served and the man standing with a large full basket behind him started to look impatient and threatening. Paul waited until all the food items in front of him had moved along the moving belt. It was almost unbearably warm because of the building's not very effective air conditioning. At that point the man grew impatient and screamed into Paul's ear.

'Come on, you idiot, get on with it and put your things on the belt.'

The mature reaction to this idiotic provocation would have been to completely ignore it. But Paul was not in a mature or normal state of mind though in the professional world he knew so well he was as mature as it is humanly possible to be.

He felt a familiar tingling in the back of his head, but this time it was quite a painful and distinctly unpleasant sensation. Then he let rip.

'Why don't you fuck off, you stupid arsehole!'

This was hardly appropriate language for a distinguished medical Professor, in fact for anyone at all, especially in a public arena. But he felt he was being controlled by an external force and had no ability to restrain himself. Besides, the man was indeed an arsehole.

The abusive man, probably in his late fifties, small, quite slim, and muscular with a mass of curly grey hair, appeared totally shocked by this ultra-strong response. After a delay of a few seconds, he responded in kind.

'Who are you calling an arsehole, you giant prick!' he screamed to Paul.

'I am calling you … who the hell do you think you are?'

'You're just too slow—'

'Bullshit. You don't tell me what to do, you pathetic idiot. I will move when I am ready and not when you tell me to.'

And so, the trading of insults went on for another minute during which Paul transfixed the man with an extremely menacing stare. He didn't know himself that he was capable of such naked aggression.

Then, quite suddenly, the man looked sideways and stopped all further verbal insults, either because he was frightened of being physically attacked by Paul or because he realised that he was totally in the wrong. Or perhaps he just stopped because he stopped.

*

This short episode of extreme verbal abuse was soon in the very recent past as Paul walked out of the building and literally ran home with the milk for their home. When he arrived home and recounted the events of what had just happened to Jane, she did not judge him in any way but just asked him how he was feeling, and, critically, whether he'd had any associated symptoms when he lost his temper. He replied that he hadn't, or at least so far as he knows he just got angry with a ghastly aggressive bully, and he just wasn't having any of it. He felt it was that simple. But both he and Jane knew full well that during the entire twenty-one-year duration of their marriage he had never lost his temper in public like that. Something was clearly wrong, she thought as she was a perceptive and caring woman. The question was what exactly was going on with her husband. Or perhaps there was nothing physically wrong with him at all and it was just the pressure of work that had finally taken its toll on her kind and clever husband. It also occurred to her that perhaps Paul had an intrinsic tendency to violent behaviour that he'd always managed to keep under control, at least until then. If that were true, it would probably be even more frightening for her than if he had some kind of mental or physical diseases. The TV interview had apparently gone very well, so that could not possibly be the cause of his atypical outburst of anger. But one thing she knew for certain. He needed help, and very soon.

CHAPTER 9

AN ANSWER OF SORTS

In a small but well-proportioned fifth floor office in the hospital's new outpatient block, two eminent consultant physicians are talking to each other in serious and hushed tones. One of these is Dr John Rapello, a charming and brilliant neurologist with an excellent reputation, and the other is Dr Monica Gowling, a senior and well-respected NHS dermatologist who is also the clinical lead in her specialty, as well as being a good friend and colleague of Paul Sellner-Smith. As their ominous conversation continues in John's office, Monica can't help shaking her head in a show of disbelief at what had only just come to light.

'But why didn't he realise something awful was going on inside his head?' she asked her colleague.

John Rapello gave a brief shrug of his slim shoulders and gave the best answer he could. 'Monica, the truth is I just don't know … maybe Paul knew something was badly wrong but just ignored or suppressed it.'

'In case it might just go away perhaps. I've seen many patients do exactly that.' John agreed.

'People sometimes forget that we doctors are just the same as everyone else when it comes to illnesses. We're just as likely to get ill but I guess we're also more likely to ignore the warning signs, the so-called red flags all of us are always told to look out for.'

'Yes … as though it could never happen to us,' she added.

'That's exactly right. It probably comes from fear and too much knowledge.'

'You mean doctors know just about everything that could happen in the worst-case scenario, and they just prefer not to think about it. So, they just blank it out of their minds?'

'Yes, that's probably right. At least it makes sense. But who knows?'

They both shook their heads in a gesture of mutual despair and grim acceptance.

Monica got up from her comfortable chair and looked wistfully out of the one large window that allowed some natural light into the room. She then turned round to John before speaking. 'So, what can you tell me about Paul's tumour?'

John arose from his swivel chair, looked very serious, which was rather unusual for him as he is normally an extremely jovial character, seemed to look dreamily into the distance, and then explained the situation as he saw it to his friend and colleague.

'Well, you know he might have gone on for many more months having these explosive episodes and accidents were it not for his wife Jane who contacted me a week ago.'

'Yes,' Monica agreed, 'that was fortunate for everyone – good for Paul and maybe even better for his patients.'

'Yes, that's true, but there are two unusual features here. First, Paul is a top cancer specialist yet completely ignored all his own symptoms which he would have immediately recognised in one of his patients. Second, as far as I have been able to see, based on the few computerised notes I've seen and also from my initial discussions with his junior and senior oncology colleagues, his management of his cancer patients had not been affected in the least. His treatment of them had been exemplary throughout.'

'That's as may be,' added Monica, 'but believe me when one or two of his patients find out that their brilliant Professor has been suffering from a malignant brain tumour for several months, the lawyer's letters are bound to follow.'

'Not necessarily, Monica, not necessarily. You know Paul is a very nice and compassionate man who was greatly liked by his patients, all of whom he genuinely cared for. In my experience of these things, such as it is, patients tend to be reluctant to sue their doctors if they like them, even when they are less than competent. And let's face it, Paul was, I mean is, the very best of the bunch and had huge expertise in his field.'

'Agreed. It's all so tragic. But please, do go on, John.'

John continued his thoughts.

'So I think from what I gathered from Paul himself and his wife Jane, who urgently referred him to me, that his brain problem had probably been going on for at least six months.'

'That long?' Monica interjected.

'Yes, I think that's very likely. Over these last few months, he's displayed the type of behaviour in his personal life that is totally atypical of his previous character. He has been more aggressive than usual, and even had a major altercation with another man in a supermarket only two weeks ago. He has been violent in the home towards his own possessions though never towards any member of his family. He has also been suffering from bad morning headaches recently and managed to crash his new Mercedes. I just wonder whether he blacked out or else had a form of seizure that made him lose all awareness and concentration for a second or two.'

'Well,' said Monica, 'I guess that would be all it takes. I am surprised he wasn't prosecuted for careless driving.'

'Well you know Paul can be very charming when he wants to, and also one shouldn't ignore the effect on people of knowing just how eminent he is.'

'It was ever thus.'

'Maybe,' replied John, 'but what is so extraordinary is that his illness seems to have had no effect at all on the high quality of either his clinical work or scientific activity. His professional work remained unscathed despite his personal life going progressively to pieces.

Also, Jane told me that sometimes he seemed to have difficulty with his actual thought processes and always doubted everything that most people would take for granted. She also suspects that once he may even have attempted to take his own life.'

'You say that, but I've since heard that Paul got pretty paranoid about some of the other consultants in the Oncology Unit.'

'Well Monica, you know what they say – just because someone is paranoid does not necessarily mean that people aren't plotting against them!'

At this John gave the full-throated version of his trademark machine gun laugh, something that tended to be infectious.

'You have a point there, John, I must admit. And I heard that the department he's in has a couple of right bastards. No names if you please.'

'Yes, I had heard all about that episode. Actually, I rather doubt that has anything to do with Paul's illness. It's more likely just another example of people behaving like some nasty people do.'

'Maybe, but I still think he may have over-reacted. Anyway, tell me about the biopsy result.'

'Well, as you know, the CT brain scan showed a

large malignant-looking mass in the right frontal region with just a suggestion of some midline shift due to cerebral oedema, findings which would certainly account for his clinical picture. The neurosurgeons did an urgent craniotomy and biopsied the tumour, which they had no hope of removing, and I heard just last night that the histology shows it to be a highly malignant glioblastoma multiforme, or grade 4 astrocytoma.'

'Ugh. Poor Paul.'

'Indeed, I couldn't have put it better myself.'

'So what about the prognosis? Remember I'm just a humble dermatologist.'

'Well of course every patient is different and there's a chance he might prove to be an outlier, but overall I reckon he would be lucky to live more than a year from now even with cranial radiotherapy.'

'Oh God, that sounds awful, John.'

John agreed.

'Exactly so, it is. I am due to speak to him this afternoon and will tell him the score. I have a feeling he'll be pretty brave and take it philosophically, if you know what I mean.'

'Yes, of course. I think you're probably right based

on my knowledge of his character as a friend and colleague.'

John looked wistfully into an imaginary distance, to an expanse of space and time beyond the large office window.

'The really remarkable thing here is how he was able to live two completely separate lives. In the workplace he was his usual stellar and highly professional self, yet at home he dissociated himself from this professional role and went completely to pieces.'

'Yes, and when he eventually lost his self-identification as a family member, he also lost that other professional role well. I guess at that point he was finished.'

'Yes,' agreed John, 'completely finished as a doctor and as a person.'

*

One week after the above conversation took place, Paul was resting at home in his favourite armchair in their downstairs living room. As he contemplated all that had happened to him over the previous few months, he experienced some comfort from the influx of life-affirming sunlight that filtered through the room's glass windows and bathed him in its warm and gentle light rays. He asked himself how it had all come to this. But at least he no longer had to suffer these severe morning headaches, due no doubt to that fact that he was taking the corticosteroid dexamethasone which had quickly resolved the cerebral oedema that was a major contributor to his symptoms. He realised from his current sense of well-being just how well he'd been before.

Most people would have been deeply shocked and indeed flawed to the point of personal decompensation – even disintegration – after learning that they had been suffering from a malignant brain tumour for several months and would probably be dead within a year or so. But that is not how Paul reacted. It was not so much that he was being brave about it, but more that he experienced a curious sense of relief that all that had gone wrong recently in his working and home life had a definite cause, and one that was both tangible and believable.

Until very recently he'd been worrying about so many different aspects of his life, from his increasing and inexplicable alienation from his loving family to the hypersensitivity to some of his so-called colleagues in the work place whose pathetic shenanigans he would normally have treated with the utter contempt they deserved. Then there were his uncontrollable outbursts of temper and even violence, both to himself and to his most treasured possessions. Only a grossly deranged person would stoop to that, and certainly not a distinguished medical Professor. Having said that, he certainly knew of one or two eminent men of science who had the maturity of a group of toddlers, while simultaneously possessing the brains of geniuses. So he mustn't generalise about human behaviour, which is as variable as the world is diverse.

His greatest problem, however, has been his hitherto inexplicable difficulty to be sure about anything at all, and his constant doubting of everything he encounters. He has literally craved certainty in his clinical work, his scientific investigations, and, most important of all, his home life. It is true that the answer came from the finding of a malignant brain tumour. While this is hardly the news he wanted to hear, nevertheless it did provide a clear answer.

It was the worst possible answer. But at least it was an answer.

ABOUT THE AUTHOR

Peter Kennedy CBE, MD, PhD, DSc is a distinguished clinician and scientist who held the Burton Chair of Neurology for 29 years (1987-2016) at the University of Glasgow where he remains active in research and teaching as an Honorary Senior Research Fellow in the Institute of Infection, Immunity and Inflammation. He also has two Masters degrees in Philosophy, and has written seven previous novels, an award winning popular science book on African Sleeping sickness, and co-edited two textbooks on neurological infections. He is a fellow of both the Royal Society of Edinburgh and the Academy of Medical Sciences.

BY THE SAME AUTHOR

ALSO AVAILABLE ON AMAZON:

TWO CENTURIES OF DOUBT (2021)
THE IMAGE IN MY MIND (2020)
ARCADIAN MEMORIES AND OTHER POEMS (2020)
THE FATAL SLEEP (2019) - Luath Press, 3rd Edition
TWELVE MONTHS OF FREEDOM (2019)
CATAPULT IN TIME (2018)
RETURN OF THE CIRCLE (2017)
BROTHERS IN RETRIBUTION (2015)
REVERSAL OF DAVID (2014)

www.ingramcontent.com/pod-product-compliance
Lightning Source LLC
LaVergne TN
LVHW010611160826
845677LV00013B/3364

* 9 7 9 8 4 9 4 5 9 0 0 9 1 *